WHERE THERE IS A WILL
THERE IS A WAY

Gordon heard the key click in the lock. He sprang to the door.

"Aunt Mary—Aunt Mary!" he called.

There was no answer—nothing save the sound of his aunt's heavy boots clattering down the back stairs.

Gordon sat down on a broken-backed chair and looked grim. He knew, as he expressed it, what he was up against. Aunt Mary had evidently determined that he should not take part in the debate. And he had promised Mr. Leckie that he would be there without fail.

He felt no particular indignation against Aunt Mary. It was just what he might have expected, and he should have been on his guard. Anyway, he had no time or energy to waste in being angry. The first thing to do was to find a way to escape and keep his promise. Nevertheless, he felt that Aunt Mary had not treated him fairly. She had never forbidden him to take part in the debate, although she let it be seen plainly that she thought it all rank foolishness. And now, when he had run down the hall to the little box-room to look for a certain book, she had snatched the chance to lock him in. Aunt Mary did things like that.

AGAINST THE ODDS

L. M. Montgomery

Against the Odds

TALES OF ACHIEVEMENT

edited by Rea Wilmshurst

BANTAM BOOKS
New York • Toronto • London • Sydney • Auckland

All of the characters in this book are fictitious
and any resemblance to actual persons living
or dead is purely coincidental.

RL 6.9, age 12 and up

AGAINST THE ODDS

A Bantam Book / published by arrangement
with McClelland & Stewart Inc.

PRINTING HISTORY

McClelland & Stewart Inc.
edition published 1993
Bantam edition published December 1994

The Starfire logo is a registered trademark of Bantam Books, a division of
Bantam Doubleday Dell Publishing Group, Inc.
Registered in U.S. Patent and Trademark Office and elsewhere.

ISBN 0-553-56592-3

Bantam Books are published by Bantam Books, a division of Bantam
Doubleday Dell Publishing Group, Inc. Its trademark, consisting of the
words "Bantam Books" and the portrayal of a rooster, is Registered
in U.S. Patent and Trademark Office and in other countries. Marca
Registrada. Bantam Books, 1540 Broadway, New York, New York 10036.

PRINTED IN THE UNITED STATES OF AMERICA

OPM　　　　　　　　　　　　　　　　　5　4　3　2　1

3 5000 00000 1130

Contents

Introduction

L. M. MONTGOMERY succeeded in establishing a place for herself in the world of letters, and her appreciation of the determination, honesty, and imagination with which people conquer the obstacles to their dreams and ambitions threads its way through the stories chosen for this collection. The "odds" present themselves in many forms in these tales. An obstacle to success or happiness may lie in one's own character: one girl has to conquer the "little leaven of easy-going selfishness in [her] nature." Or it may lie in the prejudice of someone else: a potential employer may distrust a person's heredity (several boys' fathers have bad reputations), or a guardian may refuse to sponsor more education. Some of the people in these tales are concerned specifically with getting jobs to earn money, important to them for both survival and independence; some seek higher education (often a financial problem too); others long to gain a measure of self-respect.

There are various obstacles that are overcome in this collection, but a reader will find in it more than just Horatio Alger "success" stories. Montgomery uses all her recognized talents to give her unmistakable touch of life to these tales. As always, her plots are well constructed and the resolutions are very different; her characters are real people who live with us, however briefly. She takes us to western Canada as well as to her beloved Prince Edward Island; and all locales, whether eastern farmyard or western ranch, seascape or prairie, idyllic in summer sun or bleak in drenching autumn rain, are given a reality that is distinctively hers.

The most common occupation for women in Montgomery's time was schoolteaching, a respectable though just barely self-supporting career. A year or two of training was sufficient: Anne does her two-year course in one year in *Anne of Green Gables*; Montgomery herself had only one year at Dalhousie Ladies' College besides her teacher-training. Esther Maxwell, the schoolteacher in "Why Mr. Cropper Changed His Mind," has achieved her education and has a job, but her position is jeopardized by two obstreperous boys who won't behave in school. However, Esther has grit and gumption; she takes a rather unusual course in order to tame them.

Careers were also opening up for women in writing and journalism. Montgomery draws on her own experience as a newspaper reporter in "A Substitute Journalist": Patty Baxter would love the job on a newspaper that her brother Clifford has, but she must find a way to prove herself before she can even be considered for employment – "such a thing had [never] been heard of in Aylmer." The more significant side of Montgomery's writing career is reflected in "At the Bay Shore Farm": Frances Newbury wants to write, but not for a newspaper; she aspires to being a novelist like her idol, Sara Beaumont. Mrs. Beaumont tells her that "it means perseverance and patience and much hard work. Prepare yourself for that, Frances, and one day you will win your place." If Frances can overcome those odds, she may achieve her dream.

Teaching and writing were fields Montgomery was familiar with. Acting was not. But in "Their Girl Josie" she gives a vivid picture of the obstacles against which an aspiring actress must struggle. Josie Morgan's father married an actress against his parents' wishes. When both he and his wife died, Josie came to live with her father's parents, and their prejudices against her mother and against the profession of acting seem likely to thwart her inherited theatrical instincts. (Incidentally, in only one other story that I know of, "The Great Actor's Part," published in *Canadian Courier*, 17 July 1909, did Montgomery write about acting.)

These girls are young, just beginning life and work. But overcoming obstacles and looking for jobs doesn't end with adolescence. Montgomery can be counted upon for many sympathetic portraits of "old maids," and in this collection we meet Aunt Patty, who has been keeping house out west for her brother ("The Genesis of the Doughnut Club"). When he dies, she thinks she will have to return to living in the east with her other brother and her sister-in-law: "William and Susanna were kind to me, but I was just the old maid sister, of no importance to anybody, and I never felt as if I were really living. I was simply vegetating on. . . . I wanted to stay in Carleton. . . . I loved the whole big, breezy golden west, with the rush and tingle of its young life." She hasn't the income to continue to live there, however, and what can a woman of forty-five do to earn her living?

Some of the young people in these tales are orphans and have to make their ways alone in the world; some live with widowed mothers who are financially unable to help them or even dependent upon their earnings. Willard and Sara Sheldon's father died when Willard was twelve and Sara eleven; their mother died two years before "The Blue North Room" begins. Now nineteen and eighteen, Willard and Sara have two younger siblings' futures to plan and provide for, but at this moment their most pressing problem is, where is Aunt Josephina to sleep if she comes to visit? Another pair of orphans are the twins Murray and Prue Melville, who live on one of their Uncle Abimelech's farms. Their father, Abimelech's brother, died recently, and their mother died before they could remember her. Uncle Abimelech is against higher education for both the twins, although he concedes that Prue "would make a capital lawyer" after she makes an eloquent, though unsuccessful, plea for financial help for both of them ("A Patent Medicine Testimonial").

The loss of both parents is a major one. To lose only a father might seem a lesser calamity; though, if he has left no money, the children are faced with an immediate need: they must find ways to help the family. Dorinda's widowed mother has five other children; her rich brother-in-law refuses to have anything to do with the family, and it devolves on Dorinda to find a solution to their poverty ("Dorinda's Desperate Deed"). Ned Allen's father is not mentioned, but since Ned says that his mother can't afford to send him to business college, we assume that the father is dead ("Ned's Stroke of Business"). Clifford and Patty Baxter's father died when they were sixteen and seventeen respectively, and "the failure of the company in which Mrs. Baxter's money was invested had left the little family dependent on their own resources" ("A Substitute Journalist"). Lilian Mitchell's father "had died the preceding spring" suddenly and unexpectedly, and his death brought his wife and daughter "financial ruin"; "Mrs. Mitchell was a delicate woman, and the burden of their situation fell on Lilian's young shoulders" ("Lilian's Business Venture").

These characters achieve their goals and find niches for themselves thanks to their determination and energy. But if a father has not only died penniless but also left behind an unsavoury reputation, his offspring face a much worse situation and much more is demanded of them. Besides finding jobs, they have to prove themselves in the face of ingrained prejudice against them because of their fathers. Ellis Duncan's father "had lounged, borrowed, and shirked through life"; Ellis has to convince his uncle that he is reliable ("The Fillmore Elderberries"). Gordon Holland's aunt won't help him continue his education because of his father: "Your father never kept a promise – *that* I know to my cost. And he sat down and wept over every little difficulty." She has to be shown that Gordon has gumption and grit besides intelligence ("Where There Is a Will There Is a Way").

Having both parents alive is not necessarily a guarantee of happiness. Tommy Puffer's are no asset: he has "a slatternly mother and a drunken father" ("Bessie's Doll"). By the way, this is one of very few stories in which Montgomery portrays downright, grinding poverty, and shows that higher qualities of character can bloom in very unlikely soil. Still, most living parents pose fewer problems and, if we discount Josie's grandparents, only Merle Dimma has to deal with a parent's opposition to her wishes ("A Question of Acquaintance"). Kate's father might have been an authority figure to be opposed, but he is absent on a "prolonged threshing expedition"; her mother "was always a placid little soul, with a most enviable knack of taking everything easy." She remonstrates about Kate and her visiting cousin's wild plan to drive across 120 miles of rain-drenched prairie, but does not, or cannot, forbid the expedition ("How We Went to the Wedding").

This last-mentioned story draws on Montgomery's experiences in western Canada and makes apparent the appeal the area held for her. She spent a year in Prince Albert, Saskatchewan, when she was sixteen, and over the years wrote a couple of dozen stories set in the west. This tale takes place in 1889, just about the time Montgomery herself was in Prince Albert. Phil, the girl from the east, takes a while to become attuned to the west, but she eventually comes around: "For the first time I began to think Saskatchewan beautiful, with those far-reaching parklike meadows dotted with the white-stemmed poplars, the distant bluffs bannered with the airiest of purple hazes, and the little blue lakes that sparkled and shimmered in the sunlight on every hand." Those "far-reaching parklike meadows" and persistent autumn rain are the obstacles Kate and Phil have to conquer to reach the 120-mile-distant wedding. Kate, the twenty-eight-year-old "old maid" heroine of this tale, is one of Montgomery's delightful "spunky" women. Little fazes her: staying overnight in an Indian encampment, getting mired in a mud-hole, "puddling" in a wiggler-ridden stream to find a suitable ford; she meets every situation with cheerfulness and sang-froid.

Another character typical of the spunky "new woman" that Montgomery admired and often sketched in her works is Augusta Ashley ("In Spite of Myself"). Her step-cousin, Mr. Carslake (whose first name we never learn), is sure he won't like Gussie; she's too cool and businesslike. He much prefers his other cousin, Nellie, who "would never have troubled her dear, curly head" over business. Gussie is not only capable of business, but capable of arguing. No meek agreement with the male of the species for her. She attacks and shreds her cousin's opinions during their very first meal together. He finds it "very humiliating to be worsted by a girl – a country girl at that, who had passed most of her life on a farm! No doubt she was strong-minded and wanted to vote. I was quite prepared to believe anything of her." What worse could there be than to want to vote! Definitely a "new woman" and not one with the proper respect for a man. Nothing of "Nellie's meek admiration of all [his] words and ways"! The obstacle here is Mr. Carslake's prejudice against an intelligent woman; if he proves unable to conquer his prejudice his own happiness will be at stake. (Parenthetically, however, we may be allowed to wonder what Gussie could see in him!)

Montgomery wrote about Gussie in 1896, when the "modern woman," independent and outspoken, was much to the forefront, in life and in literature. Another "modern woman" represented in this collection comes much later in Montgomery's oeuvre, in 1929, but she is not strong-minded and opinionated, she is a flapper – chic, cheeky, and clever – and rather spoiled. Interestingly, the phrases used by her father in "A Question of Acquaintance" to describe Merle Dimma's friends are virtually the same as those Montgomery used to describe the man-stealing Nan in her 1931 novel,

A Tangled Web. Dr. Dimma "approved of none of those silky sophisticated creatures Merle ran with – snaky, hipless things, with shingle bobs, and mouths that looked as if they had been making a meal of blood, and legs that might as well be naked; who powdered their noses publicly with the engaging unconcern of a cat washing its face in the gaze of thousands." Merle's father has taken a violent dislike to the man she wants to marry; the man, his bulldog, and a marauding trio of pigs play parts in poor Dr. Dimma's eventual capitulation.

In all these stories Montgomery has created believable characters who live in a world she knew well and depicted lovingly and accurately, the small villages and towns of eastern and western Canada. Though distant from us in time, her characters have problems similar to those we have today, and their methods of solving them are not very different. Perhaps for some years in the middle of this century the path for many young people went smoothly from school to job to marriage and secure old age, but nowadays more initiative and innovation are needed if one is to find a satisfying place in the job market. Just as Montgomery's characters have to be persistent and ingenious in pursuing their goals, so young people today have to be inventive and intelligent, quick to notice a need they can fill by exercising entrepreneurial skills. Just as her "disadvantaged" characters have to do battle to prove their worth in the face of prejudice and distrust, so do we all today have to deal with rigid, even if erroneous, opinions and beliefs. Old-fashioned Montgomery may be, but out of fashion, never.

A Patent Medicine
Testimonial

OU MIGHT as well try to move the rock of Gibraltar as attempt to change Uncle Abimelech's mind when it is once made up," said Murray gloomily.

Murray is like dear old Dad; he gets discouraged rather easily. Now, I'm not like that; I'm more like Mother's folks. As Uncle Abimelech has never failed to tell me when I have annoyed him, I'm "all Foster." Uncle Abimelech doesn't like the Fosters. But I'm glad I take after them. If I had folded my hands and sat down meekly when Uncle Abimelech made known his good will and pleasure regarding Murray and me after Father's death, Murray would never have got to college – nor I either, for that matter. Only I wouldn't have minded that very much. I just wanted to go to college because Murray did. I couldn't be separated from him. We were twins and had always been together.

As for Uncle Abimelech's mind, I knew that he never had been known to change it. But, as he himself was fond of saying, there has to be a first time for everything, and I had determined that this was to be the first time for him. I hadn't any idea how I was going to bring it about; but it just had to be done, and I'm not "all Foster" for nothing.

I knew I would have to depend on my own thinkers. Murray is clever at books and dissecting dead things, but he couldn't help me out in this, even if he hadn't settled beforehand that there was no use in opposing Uncle Abimelech.

"I'm going up to the garret to think this out, Murray," I said solemnly. "Don't let anybody disturb me, and if Uncle Abimelech comes over don't tell him where I am. If I don't come down in time to get tea, get it yourself. I shall not leave the garret until I have thought of some way to change Uncle Abimelech's mind."

"Then you'll be a prisoner there for the term of your natural life, dear sis," said Murray sceptically. "You're a clever girl, Prue – and you've got enough decision for two – but you'll never get the better of Uncle Abimelech."

"We'll see," I said resolutely, and up to the garret I went. I shut the door and bolted it good and fast to make sure. Then I piled some old cushions in the window seat – for one might as well be comfortable when one is thinking as not – and went over the whole ground from the beginning.

Outside the wind was thrashing the broad, leafy top of the maple whose tallest twigs reached to the funny grey eaves of our old house. One roly-poly little sparrow blew or flew to the sill and sat there for a minute, looking at me with knowing eyes. Down below I could see Murray in a corner of the yard, pottering over a sick duck. He had set its broken leg and was nursing it back to health. Anyone except Uncle Abimelech could see that Murray was simply born to be a doctor and that it was flying in the face of Providence to think of making him anything else.

From the garret windows I could see all over the farm, for the house is on the hill end of it. I could see all the dear old fields and the spring meadow and the beech woods in the southwest corner. And beyond the orchard were the two grey barns and down below at the right-hand corner was the garden with all my sweet peas fluttering over the fences and trellises like a horde of butterflies. It was a dear old place and both Murray and I loved every stick and stone on it, but there was no reason why we should go on living there when Murray didn't like farming. And it wasn't our own, anyhow. It all belonged to Uncle Abimelech.

Father and Murray and I had always lived here together. Father's health broke down during his college course. That was one reason why Uncle Abimelech was set against Murray going to college, although Murray is as chubby and sturdy a fellow as you could wish to see. Anybody with Foster in him would be that.

18

To go back to Father. The doctors told him that his only chance of recovering his strength was an open-air life, so Father rented one of Uncle Abimelech's farms and there he lived for the rest of his days. He did not get strong again until it was too late for college, and he was a square peg in a round hole all his life, as he used to tell us. Mother died before we could remember, so Murray and Dad and I were everything to each other. We were very happy too, although we were bossed by Uncle Abimelech more or less. But he meant it well and Father didn't mind.

Then Father died – oh, that was a dreadful time! I hurried over it in my thinking-out. Of course when Murray and I came to look our position squarely in the face we found that we were dependent on Uncle Abimelech for everything, even the roof over our heads. We were literally as poor as church mice and even poorer, for at least they get churches rent-free.

Murray's heart was set on going to college and studying medicine. He asked Uncle Abimelech to lend him enough money to get a start with and then he could work his own way along and pay back the loan in due time. Uncle Abimelech is rich, and Murray and I are his nearest relatives. But he simply wouldn't listen to Murray's plan.

"I put my foot firmly down on such nonsense," he said. "And you know that when *I* put my foot down something squashes."

It was not that Uncle Abimelech was miserly or that he grudged us assistance. Not at all. He was ready to deal generously by us, but it must be in his own way. His way was this. Murray and I were to stay on the farm, and when Murray was twenty-one Uncle Abimelech said he would deed the farm to him – make him a present of it out and out.

"It's a good farm, Murray," he said. "Your father never made more than a bare living out of it because he wasn't strong enough to work it properly – that's what *he* got out of a college course, by the way. But you are strong enough and ambitious enough to do well."

But Murray couldn't be a farmer, that was all there was to it. I told Uncle Abimelech so, firmly, and I talked to him for days about it, but Uncle Abimelech never wavered. He sat and listened to me with a quizzical smile on that handsome, clean-shaven, ruddy old face of his, with its cut-granite features. And in the end he said,

"You ought to be the one to go to college if either of you did, Prue. You would make a capital lawyer, if I believed in the higher education of women; but I don't. Murray can take or leave the farm as he chooses. If he prefers the latter alternative, well and good. But he gets no help from me. You're a foolish little girl, Prue, to back him up in this nonsense of his."

It makes me angry to be called a little girl when I put up my hair a year ago, and Uncle Abimelech knows it. I gave up arguing with him. I knew it was no use anyway.

I thought it all over in the garret. But no way out of the dilemma could I see. I had eaten up all the apples I had brought with me and I felt flabby and disconsolate. The sight of Uncle Abimelech stalking up the lane, as erect and lordly as usual, served to deepen my gloom.

I picked up the paper my apples had been wrapped in and looked it over gloomily. Then I saw something, and Uncle Abimelech was delivered into my hand.

The whole plan of campaign unrolled itself before me, and I fairly laughed in glee, looking out of the garret window right down on the little bald spot on the top of Uncle Abimelech's head, as he stood laying down the law to Murray about something.

When Uncle Abimelech had gone I went down to Murray.

"Buddy," I said, "I've thought of a plan. I'm not going to tell you what it is, but you are to consent to it without knowing. I think it will quench Uncle Abimelech, but you must have perfect confidence in me. You must back me up no matter what I do and let me have my own way in it all."

"All right, sis," said Murray.

"That isn't solemn enough," I protested. "I'm serious. Promise solemnly."

"I promise solemnly, 'cross my heart,'" said Murray, looking like an owl.

"Very well. Remember that your role is to lie low and say nothing, like Brer Rabbit. Alloway's Anodyne Liniment is pretty good stuff, isn't it, Murray? It cured your sprain after you had tried everything else, didn't it?"

"Yes. But I don't see the connection."

"It isn't necessary that you should. Well, what with your sprain and my rheumatics I think I can manage it."

"Look here, Prue. Are you sure that long brooding over our troubles up in the garret hasn't turned your brain?"

"My brain is all right. Now leave me, minion. There is that which I would do."

Murray grinned and went. I wrote a letter, took it down to the office, and mailed it. For a week there was nothing more to do.

There is just one trait of Uncle Abimelech's disposition more marked than his fondness for having his own way and that one thing is family pride. The Melvilles are a very old family. The name dates back to the Norman conquest when a certain Roger de Melville, who was an ancestor of ours, went over to England with William the Conqueror. I don't think the Melvilles ever did anything worth recording in history since. To be sure, as far back as we can trace, none of them has ever done anything bad either. They have been honest, respectable folks and I think that is something worth being proud of.

But Uncle Abimelech pinned his family pride to Roger de Melville. He had the Melville coat of arms and our family tree, made out by an eminent genealogist, framed and hung up in his library, and he would not have done anything that would not have chimed in with that coat of arms and a conquering ancestor for the world.

At the end of a week I got an answer to my letter. It was what I wanted. I wrote again and sent a parcel. In three weeks' time the storm burst.

One day I saw Uncle Abimelech striding up the lane. He had a big newspaper clutched in his hand. I turned to Murray, who was poring over a book of anatomy in the corner.

"Murray, Uncle Abimelech is coming. There is going to be a battle royal between us. Allow me to remind you of your promise."

"To lie low and say nothing? That's the cue, isn't it, sis?"

"Unless Uncle Abimelech appeals to you. In that case you are to back me up."

Then Uncle Abimelech stalked in. He was purple with rage. Old Roger de Melville himself never could have looked fiercer. I *did* feel a quake or two, but I faced Uncle Abimelech undauntedly. No use in having your name on the roll of Battle Abbey if you can't stand your ground.

"Prudence, what does this mean?" thundered Uncle Abimelech, as he flung the newspaper down on the table. Murray got up and peered over. Then he whistled. He started to say something but remembered just in time and stopped. But he did give me a black look. Murray has a sneaking pride of name too, although he won't own up to it and laughs at Uncle Abimelech.

I looked at the paper and began to laugh. We did look so funny, Murray and I, in that advertisement. It took up the whole page. At the top were our photos, half life-size, and underneath our names and addresses printed out in full. Below was the letter I had written to the Alloway Anodyne Liniment folks. It was a florid testimonial to the virtues of their liniment. I said that it had cured Murray's sprain after all other remedies had failed and that, when I had been left a partial wreck from a very bad attack of rheumatic fever, the only thing that restored my joints and muscles to working order was Alloway's Anodyne Liniment, and so on.

It was all true enough, although I dare say old Aunt Sarah-from-the-Hollow's rubbing had as much to do with the cures as the liniment. But that is neither here nor there.

"What does this mean, Prudence?" said Uncle Abimelech again. He was quivering with wrath, but I was as cool as a cucumber, and Murray stood like a graven image.

"Why, that, Uncle Abimelech," I said calmly, "well, it just means one of my ways of making money. That liniment company pays for those testimonials and photos, you know. They gave me fifty dollars for the privilege of publishing them. Fifty dollars will pay for books and tuition for Murray and me at Kentville Academy next winter, and Mrs. Tredgold is kind enough to say she will board me for what help I can give her around the house, and wait for Murray's until he can earn it by teaching."

I rattled all this off glibly before Uncle Abimelech could get in a word.

"It's disgraceful!" he stormed. "Disgraceful! Think of Sir Roger de Melville – and a patent medicine advertisement! Murray Melville, what were you about, sir, to let your sister disgrace herself and her family name by such an outrageous transaction?"

I quaked a bit. If Murray should fail me! But Murray was true-blue.

"I gave Prue a free hand, sir. It's an honest business transaction enough – and the family name alone won't send us to college, you know, sir."

Uncle Abimelech glared at us.

"This must be put an end to," he said. "This advertisement must not appear again. I won't have it!"

"But I've signed a contract that it is to run for six months,"

I said sturdily. "And I've others in view. You remember the Herb Cure you recommended one spring and that it did me so much good! I'm negotiating with the makers of that and – "

"The girl's mad!" said Uncle Abimelech. "Stark, staring mad!"

"Oh, no, I'm not, Uncle Abimelech. I'm merely a pretty good businesswoman. You won't help Murray to go to college, so I must. This is the only way I have, and I'm going to see it through."

After Uncle Abimelech had gone, still in a towering rage, Murray remonstrated. But I reminded him of his promise and he had to succumb.

Next day Uncle Abimelech returned – a subdued and chastened Uncle Abimelech.

"See here, Prue," he said sternly. "This thing must be stopped. I say it *must*. I am not going to have the name of Melville dragged all over the country in a patent medicine advertisement. You've played your game and won it – take what comfort you can out of the confession. If you will agree to cancel this notorious contract of yours I'll settle it with the company – and I'll put Murray through college – and you too if you want to go! Something will have to be done with you, that's certain. Is this satisfactory?"

"Perfectly," I said promptly. "If you will add thereto your promise that you will forget and forgive, Uncle Abimelech. There are to be no hard feelings."

Uncle Abimelech shrugged his shoulders.

"In for a penny, in for a pound," he said. "Very well, Prue. We wipe off all scores and begin afresh. But there must be no more such doings. You've worked your little scheme through – trust a Foster for that! But in future you've got to remember that in law you're a Melville whatever you are in fact."

I nodded dutifully. "I'll remember, Uncle Abimelech," I promised.

After everything had been arranged and Uncle Abimelech had gone I looked at Murray. "Well?" I said.

Murray twinkled. "You've accomplished the impossible, sis. But, as Uncle Abimelech intimated – don't you try it again."

The Fillmore
Elderberries

EXPECTED as much," said Timothy Robinson. His tone brought the blood into Ellis Duncan's face. The lad opened his lips quickly, as if for an angry retort, but as quickly closed them again with a set firmness oddly like Timothy Robinson's own.

"When I heard that lazy, worthless father of yours was dead, I expected you and your mother would be looking to me for help," Timothy Robinson went on harshly. "But you're mistaken if you think I'll give it. You've no claim on me, even if your father was my half-brother – no claim at all. And I'm not noted for charity."

Timothy Robinson smiled grimly. It was very true that he was far from being noted for charity. His neighbours called him "close" and "near." Some even went so far as to call him "a miserly skinflint." But this was not true. It was, however, undeniable that Timothy Robinson kept a tight clutch on his purse-strings, and although he sometimes gave liberally enough to any cause which really appealed to him, such causes were few and far between.

"I am not asking for charity, Uncle Timothy," said Ellis quietly. He passed over the slur at his father in silence, deeply as he felt it, for, alas, he knew that it was only too true. "I expect to support my mother by hard and honest work. And I am not asking you for work on the ground of our relationship. I heard you wanted a hired man, and I have come to you, as I should have gone to any other man about whom I had heard it, to ask you to hire me."

"Yes, I do want a man," said Uncle Timothy drily. "A *man* – not a half-grown boy of fourteen, not worth his salt. I want somebody able and willing to work."

Again Ellis flushed deeply and again he controlled himself. "I am willing to work, Uncle Timothy, and I think you would find me able also if you would try me. I'd work for less than a man's wages at first, of course."

"You won't work for any sort of wages from me," interrupted Timothy Robinson decidedly. "I tell you plainly that I won't hire you. You're the wrong man's son for that. Your father was lazy and incompetent and, worst of all, untrustworthy. I did try to help him once, and all I got was loss and ingratitude. I want none of his kind around my place. I don't believe in you, so you may as well take yourself off, Ellis. I've no more time to waste."

Ellis took himself off, his ears tingling. As he walked homeward his thoughts were very bitter. All Uncle Timothy had said about his father was true, and Ellis realized what a count it was against him in his efforts to obtain employment. Nobody wanted to be bothered with "Old Sam Duncan's son," though nobody had been so brutally outspoken as his Uncle Timothy.

Sam Duncan and Timothy Robinson had been half-brothers. Sam, the older, had been the son of Mrs. Robinson's former marriage. Never were two lads more dissimilar. Sam was a lazy, shiftless fellow, deserving all the hard things that came to be said of him. He would not work and nobody could depend on him, but he was a handsome lad with rather taking ways in his youth, and at first people had liked him better than the close, blunt, industrious Timothy. Their mother had died in their childhood, but Mr. Robinson had been fond of Sam and the boy had a good home. When he was twenty-two and Timothy eighteen, Mr. Robinson had died very suddenly, leaving no will. Everything he possessed went to Timothy. Sam immediately left. He said he would not stay there to be "bossed" by Timothy.

He rented a little house in the village, married a girl "far too good for him," and started in to support himself and his wife by days' work. He had lounged, borrowed, and shirked through life. Once Timothy Robinson, perhaps moved by pity for Sam's wife and baby, had hired him for a year at better wages than most hired men received in Dalrymple. Sam idled through a month of it, then got offended and left in the middle of haying. Timothy Robinson washed his hands of him after that.

When Ellis was fourteen Sam Duncan died, after a lingering illness of a year. During this time the family were kept by the charity of pitying neighbours, for Ellis could not be spared from attendance on his father to make any attempt at earning money. Mrs. Duncan was a fragile little woman, worn out with her hard life, and not strong enough to wait on her husband alone.

When Sam Duncan was dead and buried, Ellis straightened his shoulders and took counsel with himself. He must earn a livelihood for his mother and himself, and he must begin at once. He was tall and strong for his age, and had a fairly good education, his mother having determinedly kept him at school when he had pleaded to be allowed to go to work. He had always been a quiet fellow, and nobody in Dalrymple knew much about him. But they knew all about his father, and nobody would hire Ellis unless he were willing to work for a pittance that would barely clothe him.

Ellis had not gone to his Uncle Timothy until he had lost all hope of getting a place elsewhere. Now this hope too had gone. It was nearly the end of June and everybody who wanted help had secured it. Look where he would, Ellis could see no prospect of employment.

"If I could only get a chance!" he thought miserably. "I know I am not idle or lazy – I know I can work – if I could get a chance to prove it."

He was sitting on the fence of the Fillmore elderberry pasture as he said it, having taken a short cut across the fields. This pasture was rather noted in Dalrymple. Originally a mellow and fertile field, it had been almost ruined by a persistent, luxuriant growth of elderberry bushes. Old Thomas Fillmore had at first tried to conquer them by mowing them down "in the dark of the moon." But the elderberries did not seem to mind either moon or mowing, and flourished alike in all the quarters. For the past two years Old Thomas had given up the contest, and the elderberries had it all their own sweet way.

Thomas Fillmore, a bent old man with a shrewd, nutcracker face, came through the bushes while Ellis was sitting on the fence.

"Howdy, Ellis. Seen anything of my spotted calves? I've been looking for 'em for over an hour."

"No, I haven't seen any calves – but a good many might be in this pasture without being visible to the naked eye," said Ellis, with a smile.

Old Thomas shook his head ruefully. "Them elders have been too many for me," he said. "Did you ever see a worse-looking place? You'd hardly believe that twenty years ago there wasn't a better piece of land in Dalrymple than this lot, would ye? Such grass as grew here!"

"The soil must be as good as ever if anything had a chance to grow on it," said Ellis. "Couldn't those elders be rooted out?"

"It'd be a back-breaking job, but I reckon it could be done if anyone had the muscle and patience and time to tackle it. I haven't the first at my age, and my hired man hasn't the last. And nobody would do it for what I could afford to pay."

"What will you give me if I undertake to clean the elders out of this field for you, Mr. Fillmore?" asked Ellis quietly.

Old Thomas looked at him with a surprised face, which gradually reverted to its original shrewdness when he saw that Ellis was in earnest. "You must be hard up for a job," he said.

"I am," was Ellis's laconic answer.

"Well, lemme see." Old Thomas calculated carefully. He never paid a cent more for anything than he could help, and was noted for hard bargaining. "I'll give ye sixteen dollars if you clean out the whole field," he said at length.

Ellis looked at the pasture. He knew something about cleaning out elderberry brush, and he also knew that sixteen dollars would be very poor pay for it. Most of the elders were higher than a man's head, with big roots, thicker than his wrist, running deep into the ground.

"It's worth more, Mr. Fillmore," he said.

"Not to me," responded Old Thomas drily. "I've plenty more land and I'm an old fellow without any sons. I ain't going to pay out money for the benefit of some stranger who'll come after me. You can take it or leave it at sixteen dollars."

Ellis shrugged his shoulders. He had no prospect of anything else, and sixteen dollars were better than nothing. "Very well, I'll take it," he said.

"Well, now, look here," said Old Thomas shrewdly, "I'll expect you to do the work thoroughly, young man. Them roots ain't to be cut off, remember; they'll have to be dug out. And I'll expect you to finish the job if you undertake it too, and not drop it halfway through if you get a chance for a better one."

"I'll finish with your elderberries before I leave them," promised Ellis.

ELLIS WENT TO WORK the next day. His first move was to chop down all the brush and cart it into heaps for burning. This took two days and was comparatively easy work. The third day Ellis tackled the roots. By the end of the forenoon he had discovered just what cleaning out an elderberry pasture meant, but he set his teeth and resolutely persevered. During the afternoon Timothy Robinson, whose farm adjoined the Fillmore place, wandered by and halted with a look of astonishment at the sight of Ellis, busily engaged in digging and tearing out huge, tough, stubborn elder roots. The boy did not see his uncle, but worked away with a vim and vigour that were not lost on the latter.

"He never got that muscle from Sam," reflected Timothy.

"Sam would have fainted at the mere thought of stumping elders. Perhaps I've been mistaken in the boy. Well, well, we'll see if he holds out."

Ellis did hold out. The elderberries tried to hold out too, but they were no match for the lad's perseverance. It was a hard piece of work, however, and Ellis never forgot it. Week after week he toiled in the hot summer sun, digging, cutting, and dragging out roots. The job seemed endless, and his progress each day was discouragingly slow. He had expected to get through in a month, but he soon found it would take two. Frequently Timothy Robinson wandered by and looked at the increasing pile of roots and the slowly extending stretch of cleared land. But he never spoke to Ellis and made no comment on the matter to anybody.

One evening, when the field was about half done, Ellis went home more than usually tired. It had been a very hot day. Every bone and muscle in him ached. He wondered dismally if he would ever get to the end of that wretched elderberry field. When he reached home Jacob Green from Westdale was there. Jacob lost no time in announcing his errand.

"My hired boy's broke his leg, and I must fill his place right off. Somebody referred me to you. Guess I'll try you. Twelve dollars a month, board, and lodging. What say?"

For a moment Ellis's face flushed with delight. Twelve dollars a month and permanent employment! Then he remembered his promise to Mr. Fillmore. For a moment he struggled with the temptation. Then he mastered it. Perhaps the discipline of his many encounters with those elderberry roots helped him to do so.

"I'm sorry, Mr. Green," he said reluctantly. "I'd like to go, but I can't. I promised Mr. Fillmore that I'd finish cleaning up his elderberry pasture when I'd once begun it, and I shan't be through for a month yet."

34

"Well, I'd see myself turning down a good offer for Old Tom Fillmore," said Jacob Green.

"It isn't for Mr. Fillmore – it's for myself," said Ellis steadily. "I promised and I must keep my word."

Jacob drove away grumblingly. On the road he met Timothy Robinson and stopped to relate his grievances.

IT MUST BE admitted that there were times during the next month when Ellis was tempted to repent having refused Jacob Green's offer. But at the end of the month the work was done and the Fillmore elderberry pasture was an elderberry pasture no longer. All that remained of the elders, root and branch, was piled into a huge heap ready for burning.

"And I'll come up and set fire to it when it's dry enough," Ellis told Mr. Fillmore. "I claim the satisfaction of that."

"You've done the job thoroughly," said Old Thomas. "There's your sixteen dollars, and every cent of it was earned, if ever money was, I'll say that much for you. There ain't a lazy bone in your body. If you ever want a recommendation just you come to me."

As Ellis passed Timothy Robinson's place on the way home that worthy himself appeared, strolling down his lane. "Ah, Ellis," he said, speaking to his nephew for the first time since their interview two months before, "so you've finished with your job?"

"Yes, sir."

"Got your sixteen dollars, I suppose? It was worth four times that. Old Tom cheated you. You were foolish not to have gone to Green when you had the chance."

"I'd promised Mr. Fillmore to finish with his pasture, sir!"

"Humph! Well, what are you going to do now?"

"I don't know. Harvest will be on next week. I may get in somewhere as an extra hand for a spell."

"Ellis," said his uncle abruptly, after a moment's silence,

"I'm going to discharge my man. He's no earthly good. Will you take his place? I'll give you fifteen dollars a month and found."

Ellis stared at Timothy Robinson. "I thought you told me that you had no place for my father's son," he said slowly.

"I've changed my mind. I've seen how you went at that elderberry job. Great snakes, there couldn't be a better test for anybody than rooting out them things. I know you can work. When Jacob Green told me why you'd refused his offer I knew you could be depended on. You come to me and I'll do well by you. I've no kith or kin of my own except you. And look here, Ellis. I'm tired of hired housekeepers. Will your mother come up and live with us and look after things a bit? I've a good girl, and she won't have to work hard, but there must be somebody at the head of a household. She must have a good headpiece – for you have inherited good qualities from someone, and goodness knows it wasn't from your father."

"Uncle Timothy," said Ellis respectfully but firmly, "I'll accept your offer gratefully, and I am sure Mother will too. But there is one thing I must say. Perhaps my father deserves all you say of him – but he is dead – and if I come to you it must be with the understanding that nothing more is ever to be said against him."

Timothy Robinson smiled – a queer, twisted smile that yet had a hint of affection and comprehension in it. "Very well," he said. "I'll never cast his shortcomings up to you again. Come to me – and if I find you always as industrious and reliable as you've proved yourself to be negotiating them elders, I'll most likely forget that you ain't my own son some of these days."

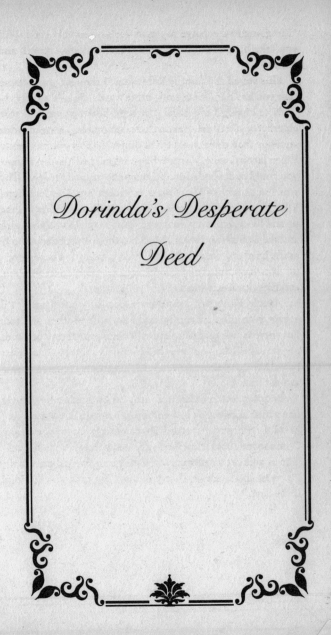

Dorinda's Desperate Deed

ORINDA had been home for a whole wonderful week and the little Pages were beginning to feel acquainted with her. When a girl goes away when she is ten and doesn't come back until she is fifteen, it is only to be expected that her family should regard her as somewhat of a stranger, especially when she is really a Page, and they are really all Carters except for the name. Dorinda had been only ten when her Aunt Mary – on the Carter side – had written to Mrs. Page, asking her to let Dorinda come to her for the winter.

Mrs. Page, albeit she was poor – nobody but herself knew how poor – and a widow with five children besides Dorinda, hesitated at first. She was afraid, with good reason, that the winter might stretch into other seasons; but Mary had lost her own only little girl in the summer, and Mrs. Page shuddered at the thought of what her loneliness must be. So, to comfort her, Mrs. Page had let Dorinda go, stipulating that she must come home in the spring. In the spring, when Dorinda's bed of violets was growing purple under the lilac bush, Aunt Mary wrote again. Dorinda was contented and happy, she said. Would not Emily let her stay for the summer? Mrs. Page cried bitterly over that letter and took sad counsel with herself. To let Dorinda stay with her aunt for the summer really meant, she knew, to let her stay altogether. Mrs. Page was finding it harder and harder to get along; there was so little and the children needed so much; Dorinda would have a good home with her Aunt Mary if she could only prevail on her rebellious mother heart to give her up. In the end she agreed to let Dorinda stay for the summer – and Dorinda had never been home since.

But now Dorinda had come back to the little white house on the hill at Willowdale, set back from the road in a smother of apple trees and vines. Aunt Mary had died very suddenly and her only son, Dorinda's cousin, had gone to Japan. There was nothing for Dorinda to do save to come home, to enter again into her old unfilled place in her mother's heart, and win a new place in the hearts of the brothers and sisters who barely remembered her at all. Leicester had been nine and Jean seven when Dorinda went away; now they were respectively fourteen and twelve.

At first they were a little shy with this big, practically brand-new sister, but this soon wore off. Nobody could be shy long with Dorinda; nobody could help liking her. She was so brisk and jolly and sympathetic – a real Page, so everybody said – while the brothers and sisters were Carter to their marrow; Carters with fair hair and blue eyes, and small, fine, wistful features; but Dorinda had merry black eyes, plump, dusky-red cheeks, and a long braid of glossy dark hair, which was perpetually being twitched from one shoulder to another as Dorinda whisked about the house on domestic duties intent.

In a week Dorinda felt herself one of the family again, with all the cares and responsibilities thereof resting on her strong young shoulders. Dorinda and her mother talked matters out fully one afternoon over their sewing, in the sunny south room where the winds got lost among the vines halfway through the open window. Mrs. Page sighed and said she really did not know what to do. Dorinda did not sigh; she did not know just what to do either, but there must be something that could be done – there is always something that can be done, if one can only find it. Dorinda sewed hard and pursed up her red lips determinedly.

"Don't you worry, Mother Page," she said briskly. "We'll be like that glorious old Roman who found a way or made it. I like overcoming difficulties. I've lots of old Admiral Page's fighting blood in me, you know. The first step is to tabulate just exactly what difficulties among our many difficulties must be ravelled out first – the capital difficulties, as it were. Most important of all comes – "

"Leicester," said Mrs. Page.

Dorinda winked her eyes as she always did when she was doubtful.

"Well, I knew he was one of them, but I wasn't going to put him the very first. However, we will. Leicester's case stands thus. He is a pretty smart boy – if he wasn't my brother, I'd say he was a very smart boy. He has gone as far in his studies as Willowdale School can take him, has qualified for entrance into the Blue Hill Academy, wants to go there this fall and begin the beginnings of a college course. Well, of course, Mother Page, we can't send Leicester to Blue Hill any more than we can send him to the moon."

"No," mourned Mrs. Page, "and the poor boy feels so badly over it. His heart is set on going to college and being a doctor like his father. He believes he could work his way through, if he could only get a start. But there isn't any chance. And I can't afford to keep him at school any longer. He is going into Mr. Churchill's store at Willow Centre in the fall. Mr. Churchill has very kindly offered him a place. Leicester hates the thought of it – I know he does, although he never says so."

"Next to Leicester's college course we want –"

"Music lessons for Jean."

Dorinda winked again.

"Are music lessons for Jean really a difficulty?" she said. "That is, one spelled with a capital?"

"Oh, yes, Dorinda dear. At least, I'm worried over it. Jean loves music so, and she has never had anything, poor child, not even as much school as she ought to have had. I've had to keep her home so much to help me with the work. She has been such a good, patient little girl too, and her heart is set on music lessons."

"Well, she must have them then – after we get Leicester's year at the academy for him. That's two. The third is a new –"

"The roof *must* be shingled this fall," said Mrs. Page

anxiously. "It really must, Dorinda. It is no better than a sieve. We are nearly drowned every time it rains. But I don't know where the money to do it is going to come from."

"Shingles for the roof, three," said Dorinda, as if she were carefully jotting down something in a mental memorandum. "And fourth – now, Mother Page, I *will* have my say this time – fourthly, biggest capital of all, a Nice, New Dress and a Warm Fur Coat for Mother Page this winter. Yes, yes, you must have them, dearest. It's absolutely necessary. We can wait a year or so for college courses and music lessons to grow; we can set basins under the leaks and borrow some more if we haven't enough. But a new dress and coat for you we must, shall, and will have, however it is to be brought about."

"I wouldn't mind if I never got another new stitch, if I could only manage the other things," said Mrs. Page stoutly. "If your Uncle Eugene would only help us a little, until Leicester got through! He really ought to. But of course he never will."

"Have you ever asked him?" said Dorinda.

"Oh, my dear, no; of course not," said Mrs. Page in a horrified tone, as if Dorinda had asked if she had ever stolen a neighbour's spoons.

"I don't see why you shouldn't," said Dorinda seriously.

"Oh, Dorinda, Uncle Eugene hates us all. He is terribly bitter against us. He would never, never listen to any request for help, even if I could bring myself to make it."

"Mother, what was the trouble between us and Uncle Eugene? I have never known the rights of it. I was too small to understand when I was home before. All I remember is that Uncle Eugene never came to see us or spoke to us when he met us anywhere, and we were all afraid of him somehow. I used to think of him as an ogre who would come creeping up the back stairs after dark and carry me off bodily if I wasn't good. What made him our enemy? And how did he come to get all of Grandfather Page's property when Father got nothing?"

"Well, you know, Dorinda, that your Grandfather Page was married twice. Eugene was his first wife's son, and your father the second wife's. Eugene was a great deal older than your father – he was twenty-five when your father was born. He was always an odd man, even in his youth, and he had been much displeased at his father's second marriage. But he was very fond of your father – whose mother, as you know, died at his birth – and they were good friends and comrades until just before your father went to college. They then quarrelled; the cause of the quarrel was insignificant; with anyone else than Eugene a reconciliation would soon have been effected. But Eugene never was friendly with your father from that time. I think he was jealous of old Grandfather's affection; thought the old man loved your father best. And then, as I have said, he was very eccentric and stubborn. Well, your father went away to college and graduated, and then – we were married. Grandfather Page was very angry with him for marrying me. He wanted him to marry somebody else. He told him he would disinherit him if he married me. I did not know this until we were married. But Grandfather Page kept his word. He sent for a lawyer and had a new will made, leaving everything to Eugene. I think, nay, I am sure, that he would have relented in time, but he died the very next week; they found him dead in his bed one morning, so Eugene got everything; and that is all there is of the story, Dorinda."

"And Uncle Eugene has been our enemy ever since?"

"Yes, ever since. So you see, Dorinda dear, that I cannot ask any favours of Uncle Eugene."

"Yes, I see," said Dorinda understandingly. To herself she added, "But I don't see why *I* shouldn't."

Dorinda thought hard and long for the next few days about the capital difficulties. She could think of only one thing to do and, despite old Admiral Page's fighting blood, she shrank from doing it. But one night she found Leicester with his head down on his books and – no, it couldn't be tears in his eyes, because Leicester laughed scornfully at the insinuation.

"I wouldn't cry over it, Dorinda; I hope I'm more of a man than *that*. But I do really feel rather cut up because I've no chance of getting to college. And I hate the thought of going into a store. But I know I must for Mother's sake, and I mean to pitch in and like it in spite of myself when the time comes. Only – only – "

And then Leicester got up and whistled and went to the window and stood with his back to Dorinda.

"That settles it," said Dorinda out loud, as she brushed her hair before the glass that night. "I'll do it."

"Do what?" asked Jean from the bed.

"A desperate deed," said Dorinda solemnly, and that was all she would say.

Next day Mrs. Page and Leicester went to town on business. In the afternoon Dorinda put on her best dress and hat and started out. Admiral Page's fighting blood was glowing in her cheeks as she walked briskly up the hill road, but her heart beat in an odd fashion.

"I wonder if I am a little scared, 'way down deep," said Dorinda. "I believe I am. But I'm going to do it for all that, and the scareder I get the more I'll do it."

Oaklawn, where Uncle Eugene lived, was two miles away. It was a fine old place in beautiful grounds. But Dorinda did not quail before its splendours; nor did her heart fail her, even after she had rung the bell and had been shown by a maid into a very handsome parlour, but it still continued to beat in that queer fashion halfway up her throat.

Presently Uncle Eugene came in, a tall, black-eyed old man, with a fine head of silver hair that should have framed a ruddy, benevolent face, instead of Uncle Eugene's hard-lipped, bushy-browed countenance.

Dorinda stood up, dusky and crimson, with brave, glowing eyes. Uncle Eugene looked at her sharply.

"Who are you?" he said bluntly.

"I am your niece, Dorinda Page," said Dorinda steadily.

"And what does my niece, Dorinda Page, want with me?" demanded Uncle Eugene, motioning to her to sit down and sitting down himself. But Dorinda remained standing. It is easier to fight on your feet.

"I want you to do four things, Uncle Eugene," she said, as calmly as if she were making the most natural and ordinary request in the world. "I want you to lend us the money to send Leicester to Blue Hill Academy; he will pay it back to you when he gets through college. I want you to lend Jean the money for music lessons; she will pay you back when she gets far enough along to give lessons herself. And I want you to lend *me* the money to shingle our house and get Mother a new dress and fur coat for the winter. I'll pay you back sometime for that, because I am going to set up as a dressmaker pretty soon."

"Anything more?" said Uncle Eugene, when Dorinda stopped.

"Nothing more just now, I think," said Dorinda reflectively.

"Why don't you ask for something for yourself?" said Uncle Eugene.

"I don't want anything for myself," said Dorinda promptly. "Or – yes, I do, too. I want your friendship, Uncle Eugene."

"Be kind enough to sit down," said Uncle Eugene.

Dorinda sat.

"You are a Page," said Uncle Eugene. "I saw that as soon as I came in. I will send Leicester to college and I shall not ask or expect to be paid back. Jean shall have her music lessons, and a piano to practise them on as well. The house shall be shingled, and the money for the new dress and coat shall be forthcoming. You and I will be friends."

"Thank you," gasped Dorinda, wondering if, after all, it wasn't a dream.

"I would have gladly assisted your mother before," said Uncle Eugene, "if she had asked me. I had determined that she must ask me first. I knew that half the money should have been your father's by rights. I was prepared to hand it over to him or his family, if I were asked for it. But I wished to humble his pride, and the Carter pride, to the point of asking for it. Not a very amiable temper, you will say? I admit it. I am not amiable and I never have been amiable. You must be prepared to find me very unamiable. I see that you are waiting for a chance to say something polite and pleasant on that score, but you may save yourself the trouble. I shall hope and expect to have you visit me often. If your mother and your brothers and sisters see fit to come with you, I shall welcome them also. I think that this is all it is necessary to say just now. Will you stay to tea with me this evening?"

Dorinda stayed to tea, since she knew that Jean was at home to attend to matters there. She and Uncle Eugene got on famously. When she left, Uncle Eugene, grim and hard-lipped as ever, saw her to the door.

"Good evening, Niece Dorinda. You are a Page and I am proud of you. Tell your mother that many things in this life are lost through not asking for them. I don't think you are in need of the information for yourself."

The Genesis of the Doughnut Club

HEN John Henry died there seemed to be nothing for me to do but pack up and go back east. I didn't want to do it, but forty-five years of sojourning in this world have taught me that a body has to do a good many things she doesn't want to do, and that most of them turn out to be for the best in the long run. But I knew perfectly well that it wasn't best for me or anybody else that I should go back to live with William and Susanna, and I couldn't think what Providence was about when things seemed to point that way.

I wanted to stay in Carleton. I loved the big, straggling, bustling little town that always reminded me of a lanky, over-grown schoolboy, all arms and legs, but full to the brim with enthusiasm and splendid ideas. I knew Carleton was bound to grow into a magnificent city, and I wanted to be there and see it grow and watch it develop; and I loved the whole big, breezy golden west, with the rush and tingle of its young life. And, more than all, I loved my boys, and what I was going to do without them or they without me was more than I knew, though I tried to think Providence might know.

But there was no place in Carleton for me; the only thing to do was to go back east, and I knew that all the time, even when I was desperately praying that I might find a way to remain. There's not much comfort, or help either, praying one way and believing another.

I'd lived down east in Northfield all my life – until five years ago – lived with my brother William and his wife. Northfield was a little pinched-up village where everybody knew more about you than you did about yourself, and you couldn't turn around without being commented upon. William and Susanna were kind to me, but I was just the old maid sister, of no importance to anybody, and I never felt as if I were really living. I was simply vegetating on, and wouldn't be missed by a single soul if I died. It is a horrible feeling, but I didn't expect it would ever be any different, and I had made up my mind that when I died I would have the word "Wasted" carved on my tombstone. It wouldn't be conventional at all, but I'd been conventional all my life, and I was determined I'd have something done out of the common even if I had to wait until I was dead to have it.

Then all at once the letter came from John Henry, my brother out west. He wrote that his wife had died and he wanted me to go out and keep house for him. I sat right down and wrote him I'd go and in a week's time I started.

It made quite a commotion; I had that much satisfaction out of it to begin with. Susanna wasn't any too well pleased. I was only the old maid sister, but I was a good cook, and help was scarce in Northfield. All the neighbours shook their heads, and warned me I wouldn't like it. I was too old to change my ways, and I'd be dreadfully homesick, and I'd find the west too rough and boisterous. I just smiled and said nothing.

Well, I came out here to Carleton, and from the time I got here I was perfectly happy. John Henry had a little rented house, and he was as poor as a church mouse, being the ne'er-do-well of our family, and the best loved, as ne'er-do-wells are so apt to be. He'd nearly died of lonesomeness since his wife's death, and he was so glad to see me. That was delightful in itself, and I was just in my element getting that little house fixed up cosy and homelike, and cooking the most elegant meals. There wasn't much work to do, just for me and him, and I got a squaw in to wash and scrub. I never thought about Northfield except to thank goodness I'd escaped from it, and John Henry and I were as happy as a king and queen.

Then after awhile my activities began to sprout and branch out, and the direction they took was *boys*. Carleton was full of boys, like all the western towns, overflowing with them as you might say, young fellows just let loose from home and mother, some of them dying of homesickness and some of them beginning to run wild and get into risky ways, some of them smart and some of them lazy, some ugly and some handsome; but all of them boys, lovable, rollicking boys, with the makings of good men in them if there was anybody to take hold of them and cut the pattern right, but liable to be spoiled just because there wasn't anybody.

Well, I did what I could. It began with John Henry bringing home some of them that worked in his office to spend the evening now and again, and they told other fellows and asked leave to bring them in too. And before long it got to be that there never was an evening there wasn't some of them there, "Aunt-Pattying" me. I told them from the start I would *not* be called Miss. When a woman has been Miss for forty-five years she gets tired of it.

So Aunt Patty it was, and Aunt Patty it remained, and I loved all those dear boys as if they'd been my own. They told me all their troubles, and I mothered them and cheered them up and scolded them, and finally topped off with a jolly good supper; for, talk as you like, you can't preach much good into a boy if he's got an aching void in his stomach. Fill *that* up with tasty victuals, and then you can do something with his spiritual nature. If a boy is well stuffed with good things and then won't listen to advice, you might as well stop wasting your breath on him, because there is something radically wrong with him. Probably his grandfather had dyspepsia. And a dyspeptic ancestor is worse for a boy than predestination, in my opinion.

Anyway, most of my boys took to going to church and Bible class of their own accord, after I'd been their aunt for awhile. The young minister thought it was all his doings, and I let him think so to keep him cheered up. He was a nice boy himself, and often dropped in of an evening too; but I never would let him talk theology until after supper. His views always seemed so much mellower then, and didn't puzzle the other boys more than was wholesome for them.

This went on for five glorious years, the only years of my life I'd ever *lived*, and then came, as I thought, the end of everything. John Henry took typhoid and died. At first that was all I could think of; and when I got so that I could think of other things, there was, as I have said, nothing for me to do but go back east.

The boys, who had been as good as gold to me all through my trouble, felt dreadfully bad over this, and coaxed me hard to stay. They said if I'd start a boarding house I'd have all the boarders I could accommodate; but I knew it was no use to think of that, because I wasn't strong enough, and help was so hard to get. No, there was nothing for it but Northfield and stagnation again, with not a stray boy anywhere to mother. I looked the dismal prospect square in the face and made up my mind to it.

But I was determined to give my boys one good celebration before I went, anyway. It was near Thanksgiving, and I resolved they should have a dinner that would keep my memory green for awhile, a real old-fashioned Thanksgiving dinner such as they used to have at home. I knew it would cost more than I could really afford, but I shut my eyes to that aspect of the question. I was going back to strict eastern economy for the rest of my days, and I meant to indulge in one wild, blissful riot of extravagance before I was cooped up again.

I counted up the boys I must have, and there were fifteen, including the minister. I invited them a fortnight ahead to make sure of getting them, though I needn't have worried, for they all said they would have broken an engagement to dine with the king for one of my dinners. The minister said he had been feeling so homesick he was afraid he wouldn't be able to preach a real thankful sermon, but now he was comfortably sure that his sermon would be overflowing with gratitude.

I just threw myself heart and soul into the preparations for that dinner. I had three turkeys and two sucking pigs, and mince pies and pumpkin pies and apple pies, and doughnuts and fruit cake and cranberry sauce and brown bread, and ever so many other things to fill up the chinks. The night before Thanksgiving everything was ready, and I was so tired I could hardly talk to Jimmy Nelson when he dropped in.

Jimmy had something on his mind, I saw that. So I said, "'Fess up, Jimmy, and then you'll be able to enjoy your call."

"I want to ask a favour of you, Aunt Patty," said Jimmy.

I knew I should have to grant it; nobody could refuse Jimmy anything, he looked so much like a nice, clean, pink-and-white little schoolboy whose mother had just scrubbed his face and told him to be good. At the same time he was one of the wildest young scamps in Carleton, or had been until a year ago. I'd got him well set on the road to reformation, and I felt worse about leaving him than any of the rest of them. I knew he was just at the critical point. With somebody to tide him over the next half year he'd probably go straight for the rest of his life, but if he were left to himself he'd likely just slip back to his old set and ways.

"I want you to let me bring my Uncle Joe to dinner tomorrow," said Jimmy. "The poor old fellow is stranded here for Thanksgiving, and he hates hotels. May I?"

"Of course," I said heartily, wondering why Jimmy seemed to think I mightn't want his Uncle Joe. "Bring him right along."

"Thanks," said Jimmy. "He'll be more than pleased. Your sublime cookery will delight him. He adores the west, but he can't endure its cooking. He's always harping on his mother's pantry and the good old down-east dinners. He's dyspeptic and pessimistic most of the time, and he's got half a dozen cronies just like himself. All they think of is railroads and bills of fare."

"Railroads!" I cried. And then an awful thought assailed me. "Jimmy Nelson, your uncle isn't – isn't – he can't be Joseph P. Nelson, the *rich* Joseph P. Nelson!"

"Oh, he's rich enough," said Jimmy, getting up and reaching for his hat. "In dollars, that is. Some ways he's poor enough. Well, I must be going. Thanks ever so much for letting me bring Uncle Joe."

And that rascal was gone, leaving me crushed. Joseph Nelson was coming to my house to dinner – Joseph P. Nelson, the millionaire railroad king, who kept his own chef and was accustomed to dining with the great ones of the earth!

I was afraid I should never be able to forgive Jimmy. I couldn't sleep a wink that night, and I cooked that dinner next day in a terrible state of mind. Every ring that came at the door made my heart jump; but in the end Jimmy didn't ring at all, but just walked in with his uncle in tow. The minute I saw Joseph P. I knew I needn't be scared of *him*; he just looked real common. He was little and thin and kind of bored-looking, with grey hair and whiskers, and his clothes were next door to downright shabbiness. If it hadn't been for the thought of that chef, I wouldn't have felt a bit ashamed of my old-fashioned Thanksgiving spread.

When Joseph P. sat down to that table he stopped looking bored. All the time the minister was saying grace that man simply stared at a big plate of doughnuts near my end of the table, as if he'd never seen anything like them before.

All the boys talked and laughed while they were eating, but Joseph P. just *ate*, tucking away turkey and vegetables and keeping an anxious eye on those doughnuts, as if he was afraid somebody else would get hold of them before his turn came. I wished I was sure it was etiquette to tell him not to worry because there were plenty more in the pantry. By the time he'd been helped three times to mince pie I gave up feeling bad about the chef. He finished off with the doughnuts, and I shan't tell how many of them he devoured, because I would not be believed.

Most of the boys had to go away soon after dinner. Joseph P. shook hands with me absently and merely said, "Good afternoon, Miss Porter." I didn't think he seemed at all grateful for his dinner, but that didn't worry me because it was for my boys I'd got it up, and not for dyspeptic millionaires whose digestion had been spoiled by private chefs. And my boys had appreciated it, there wasn't any doubt about that. Peter Crockett and Tommy Gray stayed to help me wash the dishes, and we had the jolliest time ever. Afterward we picked the turkey bones.

But that night I realized that I was once more a useless, lonely old woman. I cried myself to sleep, and next morning I hadn't spunk enough to cook myself a dinner. I dined off some crackers and the remnants of the apple pies, and I was sitting staring at the crumbs when the bell rang. I wiped away my tears and went to the door. Joseph P. Nelson was standing there, and he said, without wasting any words – it was easy to see how that man managed to get railroads built where nobody else could manage it – that he had called to see me on a little matter of business.

He took just ten minutes to make it clear to me, and when I saw the whole project I was the happiest woman in Carleton or out of it. He said he had never eaten such a Thanksgiving dinner as mine, and that I was the woman he'd been looking for for years. He said that he had a few business friends who had been brought up on a down-east farm like himself, and never got over their hankering for old-fashioned cookery.

"That is something we can't get here, with all our money," he said. "Now, Miss Porter, my nephew tells me that you wish to remain in Carleton, if you can find some way of supporting yourself. I have a proposition to make to you. These aforesaid friends of mine and I expect to spend most of our time in Carleton for the next few years. In fact we shall probably make it our home eventually. It's going to be *the* city of the west after awhile, and the centre of a dozen railroads. Well, we mean to equip a small private restaurant for ourselves and we want you to take charge of it. You won't have to do much except oversee the business and arrange the bills of fare. We want plain, substantial old-time meals and cookery. When we have a hankering for doughnuts and apple pies and cranberry tarts, we want to know just where to get them and have them the right kind. We're all horribly tired of hotel fare and fancy fol-de-rols with French names. A place where we could get a dinner such as you served yesterday would be a boon to us. We'd have started the restaurant long ago if we could have got a suitable person to take charge of it."

He named the salary the club would pay and the very sound of it made me feel rich. You may be sure I didn't take long to decide. That was a year ago, and today the Doughnut Club, as they call themselves, is a huge success, and the fame of it has gone abroad in the land, although they are pretty exclusive and keep all their good things close enough to themselves. Joseph P. took a Scotch peer there to dinner one day last week. Jimmy Nelson told me afterward that the man said it was the only satisfying meal he'd had since he left the old country.

As for me, I have my little house, my very own and no rented one, and all my dear boys, and I'm a happy old busy-body. You see, Providence did answer my prayers in spite of my lack of faith; but of course He used means, and that Thanksgiving dinner of mine was the earthly instrument of it all.

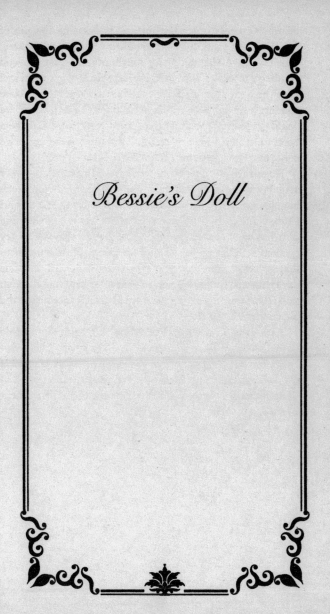

Bessie's Doll

OMMY PUFFER, sauntering up the street, stopped to look at Miss Octavia's geraniums. Tommy never could help stopping to look at Miss Octavia's flowers, much as he hated Miss Octavia. Today they were certainly worth looking at. Miss Octavia had set them all out on her verandah – rows upon rows of them, overflowing down the steps in waves of blossom and colour. Miss Octavia's geraniums were famous in Arundel, and she was very proud of them. But it was her garden which was really the delight of her heart. Miss Octavia always had the prettiest garden in Arundel, especially as far as annuals were concerned. Just now it was like faith – the substance of things hoped for. The poppies and nasturtiums and balsams and morning glories and sweet peas had been sown in the brown beds on the lawn, but they had not yet begun to come up.

Tommy was still feasting his eyes on the geraniums when Miss Octavia herself came around the corner of the house. Her face darkened the minute she saw Tommy. Most people's did. Tommy had the reputation of being a very bad, mischievous boy; he was certainly very poor and ragged, and Miss Octavia disapproved of poverty and rags on principle. Nobody, she argued, not even a boy of twelve, need be poor and ragged if he is willing to work.

"Here, you, get away out of this," she said sharply. "I'm not going to have you hanging over my palings."

"I ain't hurting your old palings," retorted Tommy sullenly. "I was jist a-looking at the flowers."

"Yes, and picking out the next one to throw a stone at," said Miss Octavia sarcastically. "It was you who threw that stone and broke my big scarlet geranium clear off the other day."

"It wasn't – I never chucked a stone at your flowers," said Tommy.

59

"Don't tell me any falsehoods, Tommy Puffer. It was you. Didn't I catch you firing stones at my cat a dozen times?"

"I might have fired 'em at an old cat, but I wouldn't tech a flower," avowed Tommy boldly – brazenly, Miss Octavia thought.

"You clear out of this or I'll make you," she said warningly.

Tommy had had his ears boxed by Miss Octavia more than once. He had no desire to have the performance repeated, so he stuck his tongue out at Miss Octavia and then marched up the street with his hands in his pockets, whistling jauntily.

"He's the most impudent brat I ever saw in my life," muttered Miss Octavia wrathfully. There was a standing feud between her and all the Arundel small boys, but Tommy was her special object of dislike.

Tommy's heart was full of wrath and bitterness as he marched away. He hated Miss Octavia; he wished something would happen to every one of her flowers; he knew it was Ned Williams who had thrown that stone, and he hoped Ned would throw some more and smash all the flowers. So Tommy raged along the street until he came to Mr. Blacklock's store, and in the window of it he saw something that put Miss Octavia and her disagreeable remarks quite out of his tow-coloured head.

This was nothing more or less than a doll. Now, Tommy was not a judge of dolls and did not take much interest in them, but he felt quite sure that this was a very fine one. It was so big; it was beautifully dressed in blue silk, with a ruffled blue silk hat; it had lovely long golden hair and big brown eyes and pink cheeks; and it stood right up in the showcase and held out its hands winningly.

"Gee, ain't it a beauty!" said Tommy admiringly. "It looks 'sif it was alive, and it's as big as a baby. I must go an' bring Bessie to see it."

Tommy at once hurried away to the shabby little street

where what he called "home" was. Tommy's home was a very homeless-looking sort of place. It was the smallest, dingiest, most slatternly house on a street noted for its dingy and slatternly houses. It was occupied by a slatternly mother and a drunken father, as well as by Tommy; and neither the father nor the mother took much notice of Tommy except to scold or nag him. So it is hardly to be wondered at if Tommy was the sort of boy who was frowned upon by respectable citizens.

But one little white blossom of pure affection bloomed in the arid desert of Tommy's existence for all that. In the preceding fall a new family had come to Arundel and moved into the tiny house next to the Puffers'. It was a small, dingy house, just like the others, but before long a great change took place in it. The new family were thrifty, industrious folks, although they were very poor. The little house was whitewashed, the paling neatly mended, the bit of a yard cleaned of all its rubbish. Muslin curtains appeared in the windows, and rows of cans, with blossoming plants, adorned the sills.

There were just three people in the Knox family – a thin little mother, who went out scrubbing and took in washing, a boy of ten, who sold newspapers and ran errands – and Bessie.

Bessie was eight years old and walked with a crutch, but she was a smart little lassie and kept the house wonderfully neat and tidy while her mother was away. The very first time she had seen Tommy she had smiled at him sweetly and said, "Good morning." From that moment Tommy was her devoted slave. Nobody had ever spoken like that to him before; nobody had ever smiled so at him. Tommy would have given his useless little life for Bessie, and thenceforth the time he was not devising mischief he spent in bringing little pleasures into her life. It was Tommy's delight to bring that smile to her pale little face and a look of pleasure into her big, patient blue eyes. The other boys on the street tried to tease Bessie at first and shouted "Cripple!" after her when she limped out. But they soon stopped it. Tommy thrashed them all one after another for it, and Bessie was left in peace. She would have had a very lonely life if it had not been for Tommy, for she could not play with the other children. But Tommy was as good as a dozen playmates, and Bessie thought him the best boy in the world. Tommy, whatever he might be with others, was very careful to be good when he was with Bessie. He never said a rude word in her hearing, and he treated her as if she were a little princess. Miss Octavia would have been amazed beyond measure if she had seen how tender and thoughtful and kind and chivalrous that neglected urchin of a Tommy could be when he tried.

Tommy found Bessie sitting by the kitchen window, looking dreamily out of it. For just a moment Tommy thought uneasily that Bessie was looking very pale and thin this spring.

"Bessie, come for a walk up to Mr. Blacklock's store," he said eagerly. "There is something there I want to show you."

"What is it?" Bessie wanted to know. But Tommy only winked mysteriously.

"Ah, I ain't going to tell you. But it's something awful pretty. Just you wait."

Bessie reached for her crutch and the two went up to the store, Tommy carefully suiting his steps to Bessie's slow ones. Just before they reached the store he made her shut her eyes and led her to the window.

"Now – look!" he commanded dramatically.

Bessie looked and Tommy was rewarded. She flushed pinkly with delight and clasped her hands in ecstasy.

"Oh, Tommy, isn't she perfectly beautiful?" she breathed. "Oh, she's the very loveliest dolly I ever saw. Oh, Tommy!"

"I thought you'd like her," said Tommy exultantly. "Don't you wish you had a doll like that of your very own, Bessie?"

Bessie looked almost rebuking, as if Tommy had asked her if she wouldn't like a golden crown or a queen's palace.

"Of course I could never have a dolly like that," she said. "She must cost an awful lot. But it's enough just to look at her. Tommy, will you bring me up here every day just to look at her?"

"'Course," said Tommy.

Bessie talked about the blue-silk doll all the way home and dreamed of her every night. "I'm going to call her Roselle Geraldine," she said. After that she went up to see Roselle Geraldine every day, gazing at her for long moments in silent rapture. Tommy almost grew jealous of her; he thought Bessie liked the doll better than she did him.

"But it don't matter a bit if she does," he thought loyally, crushing down the jealousy. "If she likes to like it better than me, it's all right."

Sometimes, though, Tommy felt uneasy. It was plain to be seen that Bessie had set her heart on that doll. And what would she do when the doll was sold, as would probably happen soon? Tommy thought Bessie would feel awful sad, and he would be responsible for it.

What Tommy feared came to pass. One afternoon, when they went up to Mr. Blacklock's store, the doll was not in the window.

"Oh," cried Bessie, bursting into tears, "she's gone – Roselle Geraldine is gone."

"Perhaps she isn't sold," said Tommy comfortingly. "Maybe they only took her out of the window 'cause the blue silk would fade. I'll go in and ask."

A minute later Tommy came out looking sober.

"Yes, she's sold, Bessie," he said. "Mr. Blacklock sold her to a lady yesterday. Don't cry, Bessie – maybe they'll put another in the window 'fore long."

"It won't be mine," sobbed Bessie. "It won't be Roselle Geraldine. It won't have a blue silk hat and such cunning brown eyes."

Bessie cried quietly all the way home, and Tommy could not comfort her. He wished he had never shown her the doll in the window.

From that day Bessie drooped, and Tommy watched her in agony. She grew paler and thinner. She was too tired to go out walking, and too tired to do the little household tasks she had delighted in. She never spoke about Roselle Geraldine, but Tommy knew she was fretting about her. Mrs. Knox could not think what ailed the child.

"She don't take a bit of interest in nothing," she complained to Mrs. Puffer. "She don't eat enough for a bird. The doctor, he says there ain't nothing the matter with her as he can find out, but she's just pining away."

Tommy heard this, and a queer, big lump came up in his throat. He had a horrible fear that he, Tommy Puffer, was going to cry. To prevent it he began to whistle loudly. But the whistle was a failure, very unlike the real Tommy-whistle. Bessie was sick – and it was all his fault, Tommy believed. If he had never taken her to see that hateful, blue-silk doll, she would never have got so fond of it as to be breaking her heart because it was sold.

"If I was only rich," said Tommy miserably, "I'd buy her a cartload of dolls, all dressed in blue silk and all with brown eyes. But I can't do nothing."

By this time Tommy had reached the paling in front of Miss Octavia's lawn, and from force of habit he stopped to look over it. But there was not much to see this time, only the little green rows and circles in the brown, well-weeded beds, and the long curves of dahlia plants, which Miss Octavia had set out a few days before. All the geraniums were carried in, and the blinds were down. Tommy knew Miss Octavia was away. He had seen her depart on the train that morning, and heard her tell a friend that she was going down to Chelton to visit her brother's folks and wouldn't be back until the next day.

64

Tommy was still leaning moodily against the paling when Mrs. Jenkins and Mrs. Reid came by, and they too paused to look at the garden.

"Dear me, how cold it is!" shivered Mrs. Reid. "There's going to be a hard frost tonight. Octavia's flowers will be nipped as sure as anything. It's a wonder she'd stay away from them overnight when her heart's so set on them."

"Her brother's wife is sick," said Mrs. Jenkins. "We haven't had any frost this spring, and I suppose Octavia never thought of such a thing. She'll feel awful bad if her flowers get frosted, especially them dahlias. Octavia sets such store by her dahlias."

Mrs. Jenkins and Mrs. Reid moved away, leaving Tommy by the paling. It was cold – there was going to be a hard frost – and Miss Octavia's plants and flowers would certainly be spoiled. Tommy thought he ought to be glad, but he wasn't. He was sorry – not for Miss Octavia, but for her flowers. Tommy had a queer, passionate love for flowers in his twisted little soul. It was a shame that they should be nipped – that all the glory of crimson and purple and gold hidden away in those little green rows and circles should never have a chance to blossom out royally. Tommy could never have put this thought into words, but it was there in his heart. He wished he could save the flowers. And couldn't he? Newspapers spread over the beds and tied around the dahlias would save them, Tommy knew. He had seen Miss Octavia doing it other springs. And he knew there was a big box of newspapers in a little shed in her backyard. Ned Williams had told him there was, and that the shed was never locked.

Tommy hurried home as quickly as he could and got a ball of twine out of his few treasures. Then he went back to Miss Octavia's garden.

The next forenoon Miss Octavia got off the train at the Arundel station with a very grim face. There had been an unusually severe frost for the time of year. All along the road

Miss Octavia had seen gardens frosted and spoiled. She knew what she should see when she got to her own – the dahlia stalks drooping and black and limp, the nasturtiums and balsams and poppies and pansies all withered and ruined.

But she didn't. Instead she saw every dahlia carefully tied up in a newspaper, and over all the beds newspapers spread out and held neatly in place with pebbles. Miss Octavia flew into her garden with a radiant face. Everything was safe – nothing was spoiled.

But who could have done it? Miss Octavia was puzzled. On one side of her lived Mrs. Kennedy, who had just moved in and, being a total stranger, would not be likely to think of Miss Octavia's flowers. On the other lived Miss Matheson, who was a "shut-in" and spent all her time on the sofa. But to Miss Matheson Miss Octavia went.

"Rachel, do you know who covered my plants up last night?"

Miss Matheson nodded. "Yes, it was Tommy Puffer. I saw him working away there with papers and twine. I thought you'd told him to do it."

"For the land's sake!" ejaculated Miss Octavia. "Tommy Puffer! Well, wonders will never cease."

Miss Octavia went back to her house feeling rather ashamed of herself when she remembered how she had always treated Tommy Puffer.

"But there must be some good in the child, or he wouldn't have done this," she said to herself. "I've been real mean, but I'll make it up to him."

Miss Octavia did not see Tommy that day, but when he passed the next morning she ran to the door and called him.

"Tommy, Tommy Puffer, come in here!"

Tommy came reluctantly. He didn't like Miss Octavia any better than he had, and he didn't know what she wanted of him. But Miss Octavia soon informed him without loss of words.

66

"Tommy, Miss Matheson tells me that it was you who saved my flowers from the frost the other night. I'm very much obliged to you indeed. Whatever made you think of doing it?"

"I hated to see the flowers spoiled," muttered Tommy, who was feeling more uncomfortable than he had ever felt in his life.

"Well, it was real thoughtful of you. I'm sorry I've been so hard on you, Tommy, and I believe now you didn't break my scarlet geranium. Is there anything I can do for you – anything you'd like to have? If it's in reason I'll get it for you, just to pay my debt."

Tommy stared at Miss Octavia with a sudden hopeful inspiration. "Oh, Miss Octavia," he cried eagerly, "will you buy a doll and give it to me?"

"Well, for the land's sake!" ejaculated Miss Octavia, unable to believe her ears. "A doll! What on earth do you want of a doll?"

"It's for Bessie," said Tommy eagerly. "You see, it's this way."

Then Tommy told Miss Octavia the whole story. Miss Octavia listened silently, sometimes nodding her head. When he had finished she went out of the room and soon returned, bringing with her the very identical doll that had been in Mr. Blacklock's window.

"I guess this is the doll," she said. "I bought it to give to a small niece of mine, but I can get another for her. You may take this to Bessie."

It would be of no use to try to describe Bessie's joy when Tommy rushed in and put Roselle Geraldine in her arms with a breathless account of the wonderful story. But from that moment Bessie began to pick up again, and soon she was better than she had ever been and the happiest little lassie in Arundel.

When a week had passed, Miss Octavia again called

Tommy in; Tommy went more willingly this time. He had begun to like Miss Octavia.

That lady looked him over sharply and somewhat dubiously. He was certainly very ragged and unkempt. But Miss Octavia saw what she had never noticed before – that Tommy's eyes were bright and frank, that Tommy's chin was a good chin, and that Tommy's smile had something very pleasant about it.

"You're fond of flowers, aren't you, Tommy?" she asked.

"You bet," was Tommy's inelegant but heartfelt answer.

"Well," said Miss Octavia slowly, "I have a brother down at Chelton who is a florist. He wants a boy of your age to do handy jobs and run errands about his establishment, and he wants one who is fond of flowers and would like to learn the business. He asked me to recommend him one, and I promised to look out for a suitable boy. Would you like the place, Tommy? And will you promise to be a very good boy and learn to be respectable if I ask my brother to give you a trial and a chance to make something of yourself?"

"Oh, Miss Octavia!" gasped Tommy. He wondered if he were simply having a beautiful dream.

But it was no dream. And it was all arranged later on. No one rejoiced more heartily in Tommy's success than Bessie.

"But I'll miss you dreadfully, Tommy," she said wistfully.

"Oh, I'll be home every Saturday night, and we'll have Sunday together, except when I've got to go to Sunday school. 'Cause Miss Octavia says I must," said Tommy comfortingly. "And the rest of the time you'll have Roselle Geraldine."

"Yes, I know," said Bessie, giving the blue-silk doll a fond kiss, "and she's just lovely. But she ain't as nice as you, Tommy, for all."

Then was Tommy's cup of happiness full.

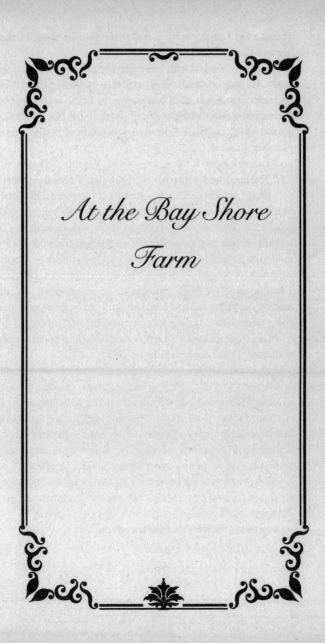

At the Bay Shore
Farm

HE NEWBURYS were agog with excitement over the Governor's picnic. As they talked it over on the verandah at sunset, they felt that life could not be worth living to those unfortunate people who had not been invited to it. Not that there were many of the latter in Claymont, for it was the Governor's native village, and the Claymonters were getting up the picnic for him during his political visit to the city fifteen miles away.

Each of the Newburys had a special reason for wishing to attend the Governor's picnic. Ralph and Elliott wanted to see the Governor himself. He was a pet hero of theirs. Had he not once been a Claymont lad just like themselves? Had he not risen to the highest office in the state by dint of sheer hard work and persistency? Had he not won a national reputation by his prompt and decisive measures during the big strike at Campden? And was he not a man, personally and politically, whom any boy might be proud to imitate? Yes, to all of these questions. Hence to the Newbury boys the interest of the picnic centred in the Governor.

"I shall feel two inches taller just to get a look at him," said Ralph enthusiastically.

"He isn't much to look at," said Frances, rather patronizingly. "I saw him once at Campden – he came to the school when his daughter was graduated. He is bald and fat. Oh, of course, he is famous and all that! But I want to go to the picnic to see Sara Beaumont. She's to be there with the Chandlers from Campden, and Mary Spearman, who knows her by sight, is going to point her out to me. I suppose it would be too much to expect to be introduced to her. I shall probably have to content myself with just looking at her."

Ralph resented hearing the Governor called bald and fat. Somehow it seemed as if his hero were being reduced to the level of common clay.

"That's like a girl," he said loftily; "thinking more about a woman who writes books than about a man like the Governor!"

"I'd rather see Sara Beaumont than forty governors," retorted Frances. "Why, she's famous – and her books are perfect! If I could ever hope to write anything like them! It's been the dream of my life just to see her ever since I read *The Story of Idlewild*. And now to think that it is to be fulfilled! It seems too good to be true that tomorrow – tomorrow, Newburys – I shall see Sara Beaumont!"

"Well," said Cecilia gently – Cecilia was always gentle even in her enthusiasm – "I shall like to see the Governor and Sara Beaumont too. But I'm going to the picnic more for the sake of seeing Nan Harris than anything else. It's three years since she went away, you know, and I've never had another chum whom I love so dearly. I'm just looking forward to meeting her and talking over all our dear, good old times. I do wonder if she has changed much. But I am sure I shall know her."

"By her red hair and her freckles?" questioned Elliott teasingly. "They'll be the same as ever, I'll be bound."

Cecilia flushed and looked as angry as she could – which isn't saying much, after all. She didn't mind when Elliott teased her about her pug nose and her big mouth, but it always hurt her when he made fun of Nan.

Nan's family had once lived across the street from the Newburys. Nan and Cecilia had been playmates all through childhood, but when both girls were fourteen the Harrises had moved out west. Cecilia had never seen Nan since. But now the latter had come east for a visit, and was with her relatives in Campden. She was to be at the picnic, and Cecilia's cup of delight brimmed over.

Mrs. Newbury came briskly into the middle of their sunset plans. She had been down to the post office, and she carried an open letter in her hand.

"Mother," said Frances, straightening up anxiously, "you have a pitying expression on your face. Which of us is it for – speak out – don't keep us in suspense. Has Mary Spearman told you that Sara Beaumont isn't going to be at the picnic?"

"Or that the Governor isn't going to be there?"

"Or that Nan Harris isn't coming?"

"Or that something's happened to put off the affair altogether?" cried Ralph and Cecilia and Elliott all at once.

Mrs. Newbury laughed. "No, it's none of those things. And I don't know just whom I do pity, but it is one of you girls. This is a letter from Grandmother Newbury. Tomorrow is her birthday, and she wants either Frances or Cecilia to go out to Ashland on the early morning train and spend the day at the Bay Shore Farm."

There was silence on the verandah of the Newburys for the space of ten seconds. Then Frances burst out with: "Mother, you know neither of us can go tomorrow. If it were any other day! But the day of the picnic!"

"I'm sorry, but one of you must go," said Mrs. Newbury firmly. "Your father said so when I called at the store to show him the letter. Grandmother Newbury would be very much hurt and displeased if her invitation were disregarded – you know that. But we leave it to yourselves to decide which one shall go."

"Don't do that," implored Frances miserably. "Pick one of us yourself – pull straws – anything to shorten the agony."

"No, you must settle it for yourselves," said Mrs. Newbury. But in spite of herself she looked at Cecilia. Cecilia was apt to be looked at, someway, when things were to be given up. Mostly it was Cecilia who gave them up. The family had come to expect it of her; they all said that Cecilia was very unselfish.

Cecilia knew that her mother looked at her, but did not turn her face. She couldn't, just then; she looked away out

73

over the hills and tried to swallow something that came up in her throat.

"Glad I'm not a girl," said Ralph, when Mrs. Newbury had gone into the house. "Whew! Nothing could induce me to give up that picnic – not if a dozen Grandmother Newburys were offended. Where's your sparkle gone now, Fran?"

"It's too bad of Grandmother Newbury," declared Frances angrily.

"Oh, Fran, she didn't know about the picnic," said Cecilia – but still without turning round.

"Well, she needn't always be so annoyed if we don't go when we are invited. Another day would do just as well," said Frances shortly. Something in her voice sounded choked too. She rose and walked to the other end of the verandah, where she stood and scowled down the road; Ralph and Elliott, feeling uncomfortable, went away.

The verandah was very still for a little while. The sun had quite set, and it was growing dark when Frances came back to the steps.

"Well, what are you going to do about it?" she said shortly. "Which of us is to go to the Bay Shore?"

"I suppose I had better go," said Cecilia slowly – very slowly indeed.

Frances kicked her slippered toe against the fern *jardinière*.

"You may see Nan Harris somewhere else before she goes back," she said consolingly.

"Yes, I may," said Cecilia. She knew quite well that she would not. Nan would return to Campden on the special train, and she was going back west in three days.

It was hard to give the picnic up, but Cecilia was used to giving things up. Nobody ever expected Frances to give things up; she was so brilliant and popular that the good things of life came her way naturally. It never seemed to matter so much about quiet Cecilia.

CECILIA CRIED HERSELF to sleep that night. She felt that it was horribly selfish of her to do so, but she couldn't help it. She awoke in the morning with a confused idea that it was very late. Why hadn't Mary called her, as she had been told to do?

Through the open door between her room and Frances's she could see that the latter's bed was empty. Then she saw a little note, addressed to her, pinned on the pillow.

Dear Saint Cecilia [it ran], when you read this I shall be on the train to Ashland to spend the day with Grand-mother Newbury. You've been giving up things so often and so long that I suppose you think you have a monopoly of it; but you see you haven't. I didn't tell you this last night because I hadn't quite made up my mind. But after you went upstairs, I fought it out to a finish and came to a decision. Sara Beaumont would keep, but Nan Harris wouldn't, so you must go to the picnic. I told Mary to call me instead of you this morning, and now I'm off. You needn't spoil your fun pitying me. Now that the wrench is over, I feel a most delightful glow of virtuous satisfaction!

Fran.

If by running after Frances Cecilia could have brought her back, Cecilia would have run. But a glance at her watch told her that Frances must already be halfway to Ashland. So she could only accept the situation.

"Well, anyway," she thought, "I'll get Mary to point Sara Beaumont out to me, and I'll store up a description of her in my mind to tell Fran tonight. I must remember to take notice of the colour of her eyes. Fran has always been exercised about that."

It was mid-forenoon when Frances arrived at Ashland station. Grandmother Newbury's man, Hiram, was waiting for her with the pony carriage, and Frances heartily enjoyed the three-mile drive to the Bay Shore Farm.

Grandmother Newbury came to the door to meet her granddaughter. She was a tall, handsome old lady with piercing black eyes and thick white hair. There was no savour of the traditional grandmother of caps and knitting about her. She was like a stately old princess and, much as her grandchildren admired her, they were decidedly in awe of her.

"So it is Frances," she said, bending her head graciously that Frances might kiss her still rosy cheek. "I expected it would be Cecilia. I heard after I had written you that there was to be a gubernatorial picnic in Claymont today, so I was quite sure it would be Cecilia. Why isn't it Cecilia?"

Frances flushed a little. There was a meaning tone in Grandmother Newbury's voice.

"Cecilia was very anxious to go to the picnic today to see an old friend of hers," she answered. "She was willing to come here, but you know, Grandmother, that Cecilia is always willing to do the things somebody else ought to do, so I decided I would stand on my rights as 'Miss Newbury' for once and come to the Bay Shore."

Grandmother Newbury smiled. She understood. Frances had always been her favourite granddaughter, but she had never been blind, clear-sighted old lady that she was, to the little leaven of easy-going selfishness in the girl's nature. She was pleased to see that Frances had conquered it this time.

"I'm glad it is you who have come – principally because you are cleverer than Cecilia," she said brusquely. "Or at least you are the better talker. And I want a clever girl and a good talker to help me entertain a guest today. She's clever herself, and she likes young girls. She is a particular friend of your Uncle Robert's family down south, and that is why I have asked her to spend a few days with me. You'll like her."

Here Grandmother Newbury led Frances into the sitting-room.

"Mrs. Kennedy, this is my granddaughter, Frances Newbury. I told you about her and her ambitions last night. You
see, Frances, we have talked you over."

Mrs. Kennedy was a much younger woman than Grandmother Newbury. She was certainly no more than fifty and,
in spite of her grey hair, looked almost girlish, so bright were
her dark eyes, so clear-cut and fresh her delicate face, and so
smart her general appearance. Frances, although not given to
sudden likings, took one for Mrs. Kennedy. She thought she
had never seen so charming a face.

She found herself enjoying the day immensely. In fact, she
forgot the Governor's picnic and Sara Beaumont altogether.
Mrs. Kennedy proved to be a delightful companion. She had
travelled extensively and was an excellent *raconteur*. She had
seen much of men and women and crystallized her experiences into sparkling little sentences and epigrams which
made Frances feel as if she were listening to one of the witty
people in clever books. But under all her sparkling wit there
was a strongly felt undercurrent of true womanly sympathy
and kind-heartedness which won affection as speedily as her
brilliance won admiration. Frances listened and laughed and
enjoyed. Once she found time to think that she would have
missed a great deal if she had not come to Bay Shore Farm that
day. Surely talking to a woman like Mrs. Kennedy was better
than looking at Sara Beaumont from a distance.

"I've been 'rewarded' in the most approved storybook
style," she thought with amusement.

In the afternoon, Grandmother Newbury packed Mrs.
Kennedy and Frances off for a walk.

"The old woman wants to have her regular nap," she told
them. "Frances, take Mrs. Kennedy to the fern walk and show
her the famous 'Newbury Bubble' among the rocks. I want to
be rid of you both until tea-time."

Frances and Mrs. Kennedy went to the fern walk and the
beautiful "Bubble" – a clear, round spring of amber-hued

water set down in a cup of rock overhung with ferns and beeches. It was a spot Frances had always loved. She found herself talking freely to Mrs. Kennedy of her hopes and plans. The older woman drew the girl out with tactful sympathy until she found that Frances's dearest ambition was some day to be a writer of books like Sara Beaumont.

"Not that I expect ever to write books like hers," she said hurriedly, "and I know it must be a long while before I can write anything worth while at all. But do you think – if I try hard and work hard – that I might do something in this line some day?"

"I think so," said Mrs. Kennedy, smiling, "if, as you say, you are willing to work hard and study hard. There will be a great deal of both and many disappointments. Sara Beaumont herself had a hard time at first – and for a very long first too. Her family was poor, you know, and Sara earned enough money to send away her first manuscripts by making a pot of jelly for a neighbour. The manuscripts came back, and Sara made more jelly and wrote more stories. Still they came back. Once she thought she had better give up writing stories and stick to the jelly alone. There did seem some little demand for the one and none at all for the other. But she determined to keep on until she either succeeded or proved to her own satisfaction that she could make better jelly than stories. And you see she did succeed. But it means perseverance and patience and much hard work. Prepare yourself for that, Frances, and one day you will win your place. Then you will look back to the 'Newbury Bubble,' and you will tell me what a good prophetess I was."

They talked longer – an earnest, helpful talk that went far to inspire Frances's hazy ambition with a definite purpose. She understood that she must not write merely to win fame for herself or even for the higher motive of pure pleasure in her work. She must aim, however humbly, to help her readers to higher planes of thought and endeavour. Then and only then would it be worth while.

"Mrs. Kennedy is going to drive you to the station," said Grandmother Newbury after tea. "I am much obliged to you, Frances, for giving up the picnic today and coming to the Bay Shore to gratify an old woman's inconvenient whim. But I shall not burden you with too much gratitude, for I think you have enjoyed yourself."

"Indeed, I have," said Frances heartily. Then she added with a laugh, "I think I would feel much more meritorious if it had not been so pleasant. It has robbed me of all the self-sacrificing complacency I felt this morning. You see, I wanted to go to that picnic to see Sara Beaumont, and I felt quite like a martyr at giving it up."

Grandmother Newbury's eyes twinkled. "You would have been beautifully disappointed had you gone. Sara Beaumont was not there. Mrs. Kennedy, I see you haven't told our secret. Frances, my dear, let me introduce you two over again. This lady is Mrs. Sara Beaumont Kennedy, the writer of *The Story of Idlewild* and all those other books you so much admire."

THE NEWBURYS were sitting on the verandah at dusk, too tired and too happy to talk. Ralph and Elliott had seen the Governor; more than that, they had been introduced to him, and he had shaken hands with them both and told them that their father and he had been chums when just their size. And Cecilia had spent a whole day with Nan Harris, who had not changed at all except to grow taller. But there was one little cloud on her content.

"I wanted to see Sara Beaumont to tell Frances about her, but I couldn't get a glimpse of her. I don't even know if she was there."

"There comes Fran up the station road now," said Ralph. "My eyes, hasn't she a step!"

Frances came smiling over the lawn and up the steps.

"So you are all home safe," she said gaily. "I hope you feasted your eyes on your beloved Governor, boys. I can tell that Cecilia forgathered with Nan by the beatific look on her face."

"Oh, Fran, it was lovely!" cried Cecilia. "But I felt so sorry – why didn't you let me go to Ashland? It was too bad you missed it – and Sara Beaumont."

"Sara Beaumont was at the Bay Shore Farm," said Frances. "I'll tell you all about it when I get my breath – I've been breathless ever since Grandmother Newbury told me of it. There's only one drawback to my supreme bliss – the remembrance of how complacently self-sacrificing I felt this morning. It humiliates me wholesomely to remember it!"

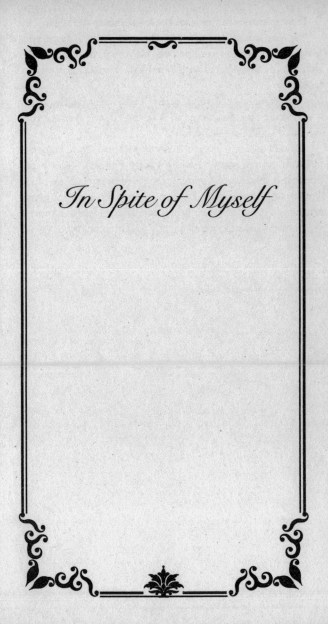

In Spite of Myself

Y TRUNK was packed and I had arranged with my senior partner – I was the junior member of a law firm – for a month's vacation. Aunt Lucy had written that her husband had gone on a sea trip and she wished me to superintend the business of his farm and mills in his absence, if I could arrange to do so. She added that "Gussie" thought it was a pity to trouble me, and wanted to do the overseeing herself, but that she – Aunt Lucy – preferred to have a man at the head of affairs.

I had never seen my step-cousin, Augusta Ashley, but I knew, from Aunt Lucy's remarks concerning her, pretty much what sort of person she was – just the precise kind I disliked immeasurably. I had no idea what her age was, but doubtless she was over thirty, tall, determined, aggressive, with a "faculty" for managing, a sharp, probing nose, and a y-formation between her eyebrows. I knew the type, and I was assured that the period of sojourn with my respected aunt would be one of strife between Miss Ashley and myself.

I wrote to Aunt Lucy to expect me, made all necessary arrangements, and went to bid Nellie goodbye. I had made up my mind to marry Nellie. I had never openly avowed myself her suitor, but we were cousins, and had grown up together, so that I knew her well enough to be sure of my ground. I liked her so well that it was easy to persuade myself that I was in love with her. She more nearly fulfilled the requirements of my ideal wife than anyone I knew. She was pleasant to look upon, without being distractingly pretty; small and fair and womanly. She dressed nicely, sang and played agreeably, danced well, and had a cheerful, affectionate disposition. She was not alarmingly clever, had no "hobbies," and looked up to me as heir to all the wisdom of the ages – what man does not like to be thought clever and brilliant? I had no formidable rival, and our families were anxious for the match. I considered myself a lucky fellow. I felt that I would be very lonely without Nellie when I was away, and she admitted frankly that she would miss me awfully. She looked so sweet that I was on the point of asking her then and there to marry me. Well, fate interfered in the guise of a small brother, so I said goodbye and left, mentally comparing her to my idea of Miss Augusta Ashley, much to the latter's disadvantage.

When I stepped from the train at a sleepy country station next day I was promptly waylaid by a black-eyed urchin who informed me that Mrs. Ashley had sent him with an express wagon for my luggage, and that "Miss Gussie" was waiting with the carriage at the store, pointing down to a small building before whose door a girl was trying to soothe her frightened horse.

As I went down the slope towards her I noticed she was tall – quite too tall for my taste. I dislike women who can look into my eyes on a level – but I had to admit that her form was remarkably symmetrical and graceful. She put out her hand – it was ungloved and large, but white and firm, with a cool, pleasant touch – and said, with a composure akin to indifference, "Mr. Carslake, I presume. Mother could not come to meet you, so she sent me. Will you be kind enough to hold my horse for a few minutes? I want to get something in the store." Whereupon she calmly transferred the reins to me and disappeared.

At the time she certainly did not impress me as pretty, yet neither could I call her plain. Taken separately, her features were good. Her nose was large and straight, the mouth also a trifle large but firm and red, the brow wide and white, shadowed by a straying dash of brown curl or two. She had a certain cool, statuesque paleness, accentuated by straight, fine, black brows, and her eyes were a bluish grey; but the pupils, as I afterward found out, had a trick of dilating into wells of blackness which, added to a long fringe of very dark lashes, made her eyes quite the most striking feature of her face. Her expression was open and frank, and her voice clear and musical without being sweet. She looked about twenty-two.

At the time I did not fancy her appearance and made a mental note to the effect that I would never like Miss Ashley. I had no use for cool, businesslike women – women should have no concern with business. Nellie would never have troubled her dear, curly head over it.

Miss Ashley came out with her arms full of packages, stowed them away in the carriage, got in, told me which road to take, and did not again speak till we were out of the village and driving along a pretty country lane, arched over with crimson maples and golden-brown beeches. The purplish haze of a sunny autumn day mellowed over the fields, and the bunch of golden rod at my companion's belt was akin to the plumed ranks along the fences. I hazarded the remark that it was a fine day; Miss Ashley gravely admitted that it was. Then a deep smile seemed to rise somewhere in her eyes and creep over her face, discovering a dimple here and there as it proceeded.

"Don't let's talk about the weather – the subject is rather stale," she said. "I suppose you are wondering why on earth Mother had to drag you away out here. I tried to show her how foolish it was, but I didn't succeed. Mother thinks there must be a man at the head of affairs or they'll never go right. I could have taken full charge easily enough; I haven't been Father's 'boy' all my life for nothing. There was no need to take you away from your business."

I protested. I said I was going to take a vacation anyway, and business was not pressing just then. I also hinted that, while I had no doubt of her capacity, she might have found the duties of superintendent rather arduous.

"Not at all," she said, with a serenity that made me groan inwardly. "I like it. Father always said I was a born business manager. You'll find Ashley's Mills very quiet, I'm afraid. It's a sort of charmed Sleepy Hollow. See, there's home," as we turned a maple-blazoned corner and looked from the crest of one hill across to that of another. "Home" was a big, white, green-shuttered house buried amid a riot of autumn colour, with a big grove of dark green spruces at the back. Below them was a glimpse of a dark blue mill pond and beyond it long sweeps of golden-brown meadow land, sloping up till they dimmed in horizon mists of pearl and purple.

"How pretty," I exclaimed admiringly.

"Isn't it?" said Gussie proudly. "I love it." Her pupils dilated into dark pools, and I rather unwillingly admitted that Miss Ashley was a fine-looking girl.

As we drove up Aunt Lucy was standing on the steps of the verandah, over whose white roof trailed a luxuriant creeper, its leaves tinged by October frosts into lovely wine reds and tawny yellows. Gussie sprang out, barely touching my offered hand with her fingertips.

"There's Mother waiting to pounce on you and hear all the family news," she said, "so go and greet her like a dutiful nephew."

"I must take out your horse for you first," I said politely.

"Not at all," said Miss Ashley, taking the reins from my hands in a way not to be disputed. "I always unharness Charley myself. No one understands him half so well. Besides, I'm used to it. Didn't I tell you I'd always been Father's boy?"

"I well believe it," I thought in disgust, as she led the horse over to the well and I went up to Aunt Lucy. Through the sitting-room windows I kept a watchful eye on Miss Ashley as she watered and deftly unharnessed Charley and led him into his stable with sundry pats on his nose. Then I saw no more of her till she came in to tell us tea was ready, and led the way out to the dining room.

It was evident Miss Gussie held the reins of household government, and no doubt worthily. Those firm, capable white hands of hers looked as though they might be equal to a good many emergencies. She talked little, leaving the conversation to Aunt Lucy and myself, though she occasionally dropped in an apt word. Toward the end of the meal, however, she caught hold of an unfortunate opinion I had incautiously advanced and tore it into tatters. The result was a spirited argument, in which Miss Gussie held her own with such ability that I was utterly routed and found another grievance against her. It was very humiliating to be worsted by a girl – a country girl at that, who had passed most of her life on a farm! No doubt she was strong-minded and wanted to vote. I was quite prepared to believe anything of her.

After tea Miss Ashley proposed a walk around the premises, in order to initiate me into my duties. Apart from his farm, Mr. Ashley owned large grist- and saw-mills and did a flourishing business, with the details of which Miss Gussie seemed so conversant that I lost all doubt of her ability to run the whole thing as she had claimed. I felt quite ignorant in the light of her superior knowledge, and our walk was enlivened by some rather too lively discussions between us. We walked about together, however, till the shadows of the firs by the mills stretched nearly across the pond and the white moon began to put on a silvery burnish. Then we wound up by a bitter dispute, during which Gussie's eyes were very black and each cheek had a round, red stain on it. She had a little air of triumph at having defeated me.

"I have to go now and see about putting away the milk, and I dare say you're not sorry to be rid of me," she said, with a demureness I had not credited her with, "but if you come to the verandah in half an hour I'll bring you out a glass of new milk and some pound cake I made today by a recipe that's been in the family for one hundred years, and I hope it will choke you for all the snubs you've been giving me." She walked away after this amiable wish, and I stood by the pond till the salmon tints faded from its waters and stars began to mirror themselves brokenly in its ripples. The mellow air was full of sweet, mingled eventide sounds as I walked back to the house. Aunt Lucy was knitting on the verandah. Gussie brought out cake and milk and chatted to us while we ate, in an inconsequent girlish way, or fed bits of cake to a green-eyed goblin in the likeness of a black cat.

She appeared in such an amiable light that I was half inclined to reconsider my opinion of her. When I went to my room the vase full of crimson leaves on my table suggested Gussie, and I repented of my unfriendliness for a moment – and only for a moment. Gussie and her mother passed through the hall below, and Aunt Lucy's soft voice floated up through my half-open door.

"Well, how do you like your cousin, my dear?"

Whereat that decided young lady promptly answered, "I think he is the most conceited youth I've met for some time."

Pleasant, wasn't it? I thought of Nellie's meek admiration of all my words and ways, and got her photo out to soothe my vanity. For the first time it struck me that her features were somewhat insipid. The thought seemed like disloyalty, so I banished it and went to bed.

I expected to dream of that disagreeable Gussie, but I did not, and I slept so soundly that it was ten o'clock the next morning before I woke. I sprang out of bed in dismay, dressed hastily, and ran down, not a little provoked at myself. Through the window I saw Gussie in the garden digging up some geraniums. She was enveloped in a clay-stained brown apron, a big flapping straw hat half hid her face, and she wore a pair of muddy old kid gloves. Her whole appearance was disreputable, and the face she turned to me as I said "Good morning" had a diagonal streak of clay across it. I added slovenliness to my already long list of her demerits.

"Good afternoon, rather. Don't you know what time it is?

The men were here three hours ago for their orders. I thought it a pity to disturb your peaceful dreams, so I gave them myself and sent them off."

I was angrier than ever. A nice beginning I had made. And was that girl laughing at me?

"I expected to be called in time, certainly," I said stiffly. "I am not accustomed to oversleep myself. I promise it will not occur again."

My dignity was quite lost on Gussie. She peeled off her gloves cheerfully and said, "I suppose you'd like some breakfast. Just wait till I wash my hands and I'll get you some. Then if you're pining to be useful you can help me take up these geraniums."

There was no help for it. After I had breakfasted I went, with many misgivings. We got on fairly well, however. Gussie was particularly lively and kept me too busy for argument. I quite enjoyed the time and we did not quarrel until nearly the last, when we fell out bitterly over some horticultural problem and went in to dinner in sulky silence. Gussie disappeared after dinner and I saw no more of her. I was glad of this, but after a time I began to find it a little dull. Even a dispute would have been livelier. I visited the mills, looked over the farm, and then carelessly asked Aunt Lucy where Miss Ashley was. Aunt Lucy replied that she had gone to visit a friend and would not be back till the next day.

This was satisfactory, of course, highly so. What a relief it was to be rid of that girl with her self-assertiveness and independence. I said to myself that I hoped her friend would keep her for a week. I forgot to be disappointed that she had not when, next afternoon, I saw Gussie coming in at the gate with a tolerably large satchel and an armful of golden rod. I sauntered down to relieve her, and we had a sharp argument under way before we were halfway up the lane. As usual Gussie refused to give in that she was wrong.

Her walk had brought a faint, clear tint to her cheeks and her rippling dusky hair had half slipped down on her neck. She said she had to make some cookies for tea and if I had nothing better to do I might go and talk to her while she mixed them. It was not a gracious invitation but I went, rather than be left to my own company.

By the end of the week I was as much at home at Ashley Mills as if I had lived there all my life. Gussie and I were thrown together a good deal, for lack of other companions, and I saw no reason to change my opinion of her. She could be lively and entertaining when she chose, and at times she might be called beautiful. Still, I did not approve of her – at least I thought so, most of the time. Once in a while came a state of feeling which I did not quite understand.

One evening I went to prayer meeting with Aunt Lucy and Gussie. I had not seen the minister of Ashley Mills before, though Gussie and her mother seemed to know him intimately. I had an idea that he was old and silvery-haired and benevolent-looking. So I was rather surprised to find him as young as myself – a tall, pale, intellectual-looking man, with a high, white brow and dark, earnest eyes – decidedly attractive.

I was still more surprised when, after the service, he joined Gussie at the door and went down the steps with her. I felt distinctly ill-treated as I fell back with Aunt Lucy. There was no reason why I should – none; it ought to have been a relief. Rev. Carroll Martin had every right to see Miss Ashley home if he chose. Doubtless a girl who knew all there was to be known about business, farming, and milling, to say nothing of housekeeping and gardening, could discuss theology also. It was none of my business.

I don't know what kept me awake so late that night. As a consequence I overslept myself. I had managed to redeem my reputation on this point, but here it was lost again. I felt cross and foolish and cantankerous when I went out.

There was some unusual commotion at the well. It was an old-fashioned open one, with a chain and windlass. Aunt Lucy was peering anxiously down its mouth, from which a ladder was sticking. Just as I got there Gussie emerged from its depths with a triumphant face. Her skirt was muddy and draggled, her hair had tumbled down, and she held a dripping black cat.

"Coco must have fallen into the well last night," she explained, as I helped her to the ground. "I missed him at milking-time, and when I came to the well this morning I heard the most ear-splitting yowls coming up from it. I couldn't think where he could possibly be, for the water was quite calm, until I saw he had crept into a little crevice in the stones on the side. So I got a ladder and went down after him."

"You should have called me," I said sourly. "You might have killed yourself, going down there."

"And Coco might have tumbled in and drowned while you were getting up," retorted Gussie. "Besides, what was the need? I could go down as well as you."

"No doubt," I said, more sharply than I had any business to. "I don't dream of disputing your ability to do anything you may take it into your head to do. Most young ladies are not in the habit of going down wells, however."

"Perhaps not," she rejoined, with freezing calmness. "But, as you may have discovered, I am not 'most young ladies.' I am myself, Augusta Ashley, and accountable to nobody but myself if I choose to go down the well every day for pure love of it."

She walked off in her wet dress with her muddy cat. Gussie Ashley was the only girl I ever saw who could be dignified under such circumstances.

I was in a very bad humour with myself as I went off to see about having the well cleaned out. I had offended Gussie and I knew she would not be easily appeased. Nor was she. For a week she kept me politely, studiously, at a distance, in spite of my most humble advances. Rev. Carroll was a frequent caller, ostensibly to make arrangements about a Sunday school they were organizing in a poor part of the community. Gussie and he held long conversations on this enthralling subject. Then Gussie went on another visit to her friend, and when she came back so did Rev. Carroll.

One calm, hazy afternoon I was coming slowly up from the mills. Happening to glance at the kitchen roof, I gasped. It was on fire in one place. Evidently the dry shingles had caught fire from a spark. There was not a soul about save Gussie, Aunt Lucy, and myself. I dashed wildly into the kitchen, where Gussie was peeling apples.

"The house is on fire," I exclaimed. Gussie dropped her knife and turned pale.

"Don't wake Mother," was all she said, as she snatched a bucket of water from the table. The ladder was still lying by the well. In a second I had raised it to the roof and, while Gussie went up it like a squirrel and dashed the water on the flames, I had two more buckets ready for her.

Fortunately the fire had made little headway, though a few minutes more would have given it a dangerous start. The flames hissed and died out as Gussie threw on the water, and in a few seconds only a small black hole in the shingles remained. Gussie slid down the ladder. She trembled in every limb, but she put out her wet hand to me with a faint, triumphant smile. We shook hands across the ladder with a cordiality never before expressed.

For the next week, in spite of Rev. Carroll, I was happy when I thought of Gussie and miserable when I thought of Nellie. I held myself in some way bound to her and – was she not my ideal? Undoubtedly!

One day I got a letter from my sister. It was long and newsy, and the eighth page was most interesting.

"If you don't come home and look after Nellie," wrote Kate, "you'll soon not have her to look after. You remember that old lover of hers, Rod Allen? Well, he's home from the west now, immensely rich, they say, and his attentions to Nellie are the town talk. I think she likes him too. If you bury yourself any longer at Ashley Mills I won't be responsible for the consequences."

This lifted an immense weight from my mind, but the ninth page hurled it back again.

"You never say anything of Miss Ashley in your letters. What is she like – young or old, ugly or pretty, clever or dull? I met a lady recently who knows her and thinks she is charming. She also said Miss Ashley was to be married soon to Rev. Something-or-Other. Is it true?"

Aye, was it? Quite likely. Kate's letter made a very miserable man of me. Gussie found me a dull companion that day. After several vain attempts to rouse me to interest she gave it up.

"There's no use talking to you," she said impatiently. "I believe you are homesick. That letter you got this morning looked suspicious. Anyhow, I hope you'll get over it before I get back."

"Are you going away again?" I asked.

"Yes. I am going to stay a few days with Flossie." Flossie was that inseparable chum of hers.

"You seem to spend a good deal of your time with her," I remarked discontentedly.

Gussie opened her eyes at my tone.

"Why, of course," she said. "Flossie and I have always been chums. And she needs me more than ever just now, for she is awfully busy. She is to be married next month."

"Oh, I see – and you –"

"I'm to be bridesmaid, of course, and we've heaps to do. Flossie wanted to wait until Christmas, but Mr. Martin is in a –"

"Mr. Martin," I interrupted. "Is Mr. Martin going to marry your friend?"

"Why, yes. Didn't you know? They just suit each other. There he comes now. He's going to drive me over, and I'm not ready. Talk to him, for pity's sake, while I go and dress."

I never enjoyed a conversation more. Rev. Carroll Martin was a remarkably interesting man.

Nellie married Rod Allen at Christmas and I was best man. Nellie made a charming little bride, and Rod fairly worshipped her. My own wedding did not come off until spring, as Gussie said she could not get ready before that.

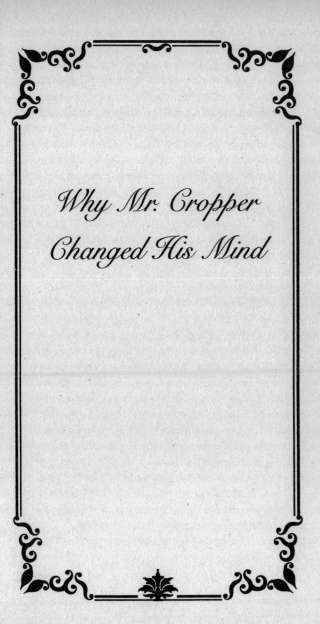

Why Mr. Cropper
Changed His Mind

WELL, Miss Maxwell, how did you get along today?" asked Mr. Baxter affably, when the new teacher came to the table.

She was a slight, dark girl, rather plain-looking, but with a smart, energetic way. Mr. Baxter approved of her; he "liked her style," as he would have said.

The summer term had just opened in the Maitland district. Esther Maxwell was a stranger, but she was a capable girl, and had no doubt of her own ability to get and keep the school in good working order. She smiled brightly at Mr. Baxter.

"Very well for a beginning. The children seem bright and teachable and not hard to control."

Mr. Baxter nodded. "There are no bad children in the school except the Cropper boys – and they can be good enough if they like. Reckon they weren't there today?"

"No."

"Well, Miss Maxwell, I think it only fair to tell you that you may have trouble with those boys when they do come. Forewarned is forearmed, you know. Mr. Cropper was opposed to our hiring you. Not, of course, that he had any personal objection to you, but he is set against female teachers, and when a Cropper is set there is nothing on earth can change him. He says female teachers can't keep order. He's started in with a spite at you on general principles, and the boys know it. They know he'll back them up in secret, no matter what they do, just to prove his opinions. Cropper is sly and slippery, and it is hard to corner him."

"Are the boys big?" queried Esther anxiously.

"Yes. Thirteen and fourteen and big for their age. You can't whip 'em – that is the trouble. A man might, but they'd twist you around their fingers. You'll have your hands full, I'm afraid. But maybe they'll behave all right after all."

Mr. Baxter privately had no hope that they would, but

Esther hoped for the best. She could not believe that Mr. Cropper would carry his prejudices into a personal application. This conviction was strengthened when he overtook her walking from school the next day and drove her home. He was a big, handsome man with a very suave, polite manner. He asked interestedly about her school and her work, hoped she was getting on well, and said he had two young rascals of his own to send soon. Esther felt relieved. She thought that Mr. Baxter had exaggerated matters a little.

"That plum tree of Mrs. Charley's is loaded with fruit again this year," remarked Mr. Baxter at the tea table that evening. "I came past it today on my way 'cross lots home from the woods. There will be bushels of plums on it."

"I don't suppose poor Mrs. Charley will get one of them any more than she ever has," said Mrs. Baxter indignantly. "It's a burning shame, that's what it is! I just wish she could catch the Croppers once."

"You haven't any proof that it is really them, Mary," objected her husband, "and you shouldn't make reckless accusations before folks."

"I know very well it is them," retorted Mrs. Baxter, "and so do you, Adoniram. And Mrs. Charley knows it too, although she can't prove it – more's the pity! I don't say Isaac Cropper steals those plums with his own hands. But he knows who does – and the plums go into Mehitable Cropper's preserving kettle; there's nothing surer."

"You see, Miss Maxwell, it's this way," explained Mr. Baxter, turning to Esther. "Mrs. Charley Cropper's husband was Isaac's brother. They never got on well together, and when Charley died there was a tremendous fuss about the property. Isaac acted mean and scandalous clear through, and public opinion has been down on him ever since. But Mrs. Charley is a pretty smart woman, and he didn't get the better of her in everything. There was a strip of disputed land between the two farms, and she secured it. There's a big plum tree growing on it close to the line fence. It's the finest one in Maitland. But Mrs. Charley never gets a plum from it."

"But what becomes of them?" asked Esther.

"They disappear," said Mr. Baxter, with a significant nod. "When the plums are anything like ripe Mrs. Charley discovers some day that there isn't one left on the tree. She has never been able to get a scrap of proof as to who took them, or she'd make it hot for them. But nobody in Maitland has any doubt in his own mind that Isaac Cropper knows where those plums go."

"I don't think Mr. Cropper would steal," protested Esther.

"Well, he doesn't consider it stealing, you know. He claims the land and says the plums are his. I don't doubt that he is quite clear in his own mind that they are. And he does hate Mrs. Charley. I'd give considerable to see the old sinner fairly caught, but he is too deep."

"I think Mr. Baxter is too hard on Mr. Cropper," said Esther to herself later on. "He has probably some private prejudice against him."

BUT A MONTH LATER she had changed her opinion. During that time the Cropper boys had come to school.

At first Esther had been inclined to like them. They were handsome lads, with the same smooth way that characterized their father, and seemed bright and intelligent. For a few days all went well, and Esther felt decidedly relieved.

But before long a subtle spirit of insubordination began to make itself felt in the school. Esther found herself powerless to cope with it. The Croppers never openly defied her, but they did precisely as they pleased. The other pupils thought themselves at liberty to follow this example, and in a month's time poor Esther had completely lost control of her little kingdom. Some complaints were heard among the ratepayers and even Mr. Baxter looked dubious. She knew that unless she could regain her authority she would be requested to hand in her resignation, but she was baffled by the elusive system of defiance which the Cropper boys had organized.

One day she resolved to go to Mr. Cropper himself and appeal to his sense of justice, if he had any. It had been an especially hard day in school. When she had been absent at the noon hour all the desks in the schoolroom had been piled in a pyramid on the floor, books and slates interchanged, and various other pranks played. When questioned every pupil denied having done or helped to do it. Alfred and Bob Cropper looked her squarely in the eyes and declared their innocence in their usual gentlemanly fashion, yet Esther felt sure that they were the guilty ones. She also knew what exaggerated accounts of the affair would be taken home to Maitland tea tables, and she felt like sitting down to cry. But she did not. Instead she set her mouth firmly, helped the children restore the room to order, and after school went up to Isaac Cropper's house.

That gentleman himself came in from the harvest field looking as courtly as usual, even in his rough working clothes. He shook hands heartily, told her he was glad to see her, and began talking about the weather. Esther was not to be turned from her object thus, although she felt her courage ebbing away from her as it always did in the presence of the Cropper imperviousness.

"I have come up to see you about Alfred and Robert, Mr. Cropper," she said. "They are not behaving well in school."

"Indeed!" Mr. Cropper's voice expressed bland surprise. "That is strange. As a rule I do not think Alfred and Robert have been troublesome to their teachers. What have they been doing now?"

"They refuse to obey my orders," said Esther faintly.

"Ah, well, Miss Maxwell, perhaps you will pardon my saying that a teacher should be able to enforce her orders. My boys are high-spirited fellows and need a strong, firm hand to restrain them. I have always said I considered it advisable to employ a male teacher in Maitland school. We should have better order. Not that I disapprove of you personally – far from it. I should be glad to see you succeed. But I have heard many complaints regarding the order in school at present."

"I had no trouble until your boys came," retorted Esther, losing her temper a little, "and I believe that if you were willing to co-operate with me that I could govern them."

"Well, you see," said Mr. Cropper easily, "when I send my boys to school I naturally expect that the teacher will be capable of doing the work she has been hired to do."

"Then you refuse to help me?" said Esther in a trembling voice.

"Why, my dear young lady, what can I do? Boys soon know when they can disobey a teacher with impunity. No doubt you will be able to secure a school easier to control and will do good work. But here, as I have already said, we need a firm hand at the helm. But you are not going yet, Miss Maxwell? You need some refreshment after your long walk. Mrs. Cropper will bring you in something."

"No, thank you," said poor Esther. She felt that she must get away at once or she would burst into heartsick tears under those steely, bland blue eyes. When she got home she shut herself up in her room and cried. There was nothing for her to do but resign, she thought dismally.

On the following Saturday Esther went for an afternoon walk, carrying her kodak with her. It was a brilliantly fine autumn day, and woods and fields were basking in a mellow haze. Esther went across lots to Mrs. Charley Cropper's house, intending to make a call. But the house was locked up and evidently deserted, so she rambled past it to the back fields. Passing through a grove of maples she came out among leafy young saplings on the other side. Just beyond her, with its laden boughs hanging over the line fence, was the famous plum tree. Esther looked at it for a moment. Then an odd smile gleamed over her face and she lifted her kodak.

Monday evening Esther called on Mr. Cropper again. After the preliminary remarks in which he indulged, she said, with seeming irrelevance, that Saturday had been a fine day.

"There was an excellent light for snapshots," she went on coolly. "I went out with my kodak and was lucky enough to get a good negative. I have brought you up a proof. I thought you would be interested in it."

She rose and placed the proof on the table before Mr. Cropper. The plum tree came out clearly. Bob and Alf Cropper were up among the boughs picking the plums. On the ground beneath them stood their father with a basket of fruit in his hand.

Mr. Cropper looked at the proof and from it to Esther. His eyes had lost their unconcerned glitter, but his voice was defiant.

"The plums are mine by right," he said.

"Perhaps," said Esther calmly, "but there are some who do not think so. Mrs. Charley, for instance – she would like to see this proof, I think."

"Don't show it to her," cried Mr. Cropper hastily. "I tell you, Miss Maxwell, the plums are mine. But I am tired of fighting over them and I had decided before this that I'd let her have them after this. It's only a trifle, anyhow. And about that little matter we were discussing the other night, Miss Maxwell. I have been thinking it over, and I admit I was somewhat unreasonable. I'll talk to Alfred and Robert and see what I can do."

"Very well," said Esther quietly. "The matter of the plums isn't my business and I don't wish to be involved in your family feuds, especially as you say that you mean to allow Mrs. Charley to enjoy her own in future. As for the school, we will hope that matters will improve."

"You'll leave the proof with me, won't you?" said Mr. Cropper eagerly.

"Oh, certainly," said Esther, smiling. "I have the negative still, you know."

From that time out the Cropper boys were models of good behaviour and the other turbulent spirits, having lost their leaders, were soon quelled. Complaint died away, and at the end of the term Esther was re-engaged.

"You seem to have won old Cropper over to your side entirely," Mr. Baxter told her that night. "He said at the meeting today that you were the best teacher we had ever had and moved to raise your salary. I never knew Isaac Cropper to change his opinions so handsomely."

Esther smiled. She knew it had taken a powerful lever to change Mr. Cropper's opinion, but she kept her own counsel.

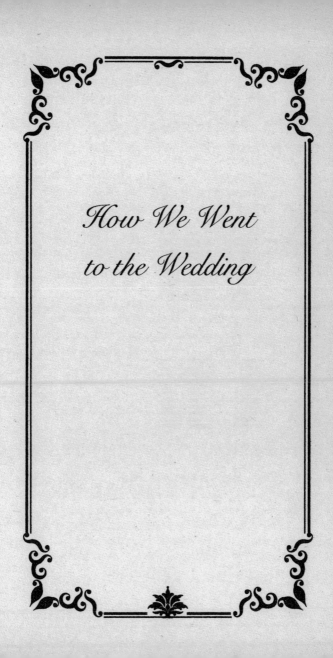

How We Went
to the Wedding

F IT WERE to clear up I wouldn't know how to behave, it would seem so unnatural," said Kate. "Do you, by any chance, remember what the sun looks like, Phil?"

"Does the sun ever shine in Saskatchewan anyhow?" I asked with assumed sarcasm, just to make Kate's big, bonny black eyes flash.

They did flash; but Kate laughed immediately after, as she sat down on a chair in front of me and cradled her long, thin, spirited dark face in her palms.

"We have more sunny weather in Saskatchewan than in all the rest of Canada put together, in an average year," she said, clicking her strong, white teeth and snapping her eyes at me. "But I can't blame you for feeling sceptical about it, Phil. If I went to a new country and it rained every day – all day – all night – after I got there for three whole weeks I'd think things not lawful to be uttered about the climate too. So, little cousin, I forgive you. Remember that 'into each life some rain must fall, some days must be dark and dreary.' Oh, if you'd only come to visit me last fall. We had such a bee-yew-tiful September last year. We were drowned in sunshine. This fall we're drowned in water. Old settlers tell of a similar visitation in '72, though they claim even that wasn't quite as bad as this."

I was sitting rather disconsolately by an upper window of Uncle Kenneth Morrison's log house at Arrow Creek. Below was what in dry weather – so, at least, I was told – was merely a pretty, grassy little valley, but which was now a considerable creek of muddy yellow water, rising daily. Beyond was a cheerless prospect of sodden prairie and dripping "bluff."

"It would be a golden, mellow land, with purple hazes over the bluffs, in a normal fall," assured Kate. "Even now if the sun were just to shine out for a day and a good 'chinook' blow

you'd see a surprising change. I feel like chanting continually
that old rhyme I learned in the first primer,

> 'Rain, rain, go away,
> Come again some other day:
> – some other day next summer –
> Phil and Katie want to play.'

Philippa, dear girl, don't look so dismal. It's bound to clear up
sometime."

"I wish the 'sometime' would come soon, then," I said,
rather grumpily.

"You know it hasn't really rained for three days," protested Kate. "It's been damp and horrid and threatening, but it
hasn't rained. I defy you to say that it has actually rained."

"When it's so wet underfoot that you can't stir out without rubber boots it might as well be wet overhead too," I said,
still grumpily.

"I believe you're homesick, girl," said Kate anxiously.

"No, I'm not," I answered, laughing, and feeling ashamed
of my ungraciousness. "Nobody could be homesick with
such a jolly good fellow as you around, Kate. It's only that this
weather is getting on my nerves a bit. I'm fit for treasons,
stratagems, and spoils. If your chinook doesn't come soon,
Kitty, I'll do something quite desperate."

"I feel that way myself," admitted Kate. "Real reckless,
Phil. Anyhow, let's put on our despised rubber boots and sally
out for a wade."

"Here's Jim Nash coming on horseback down the trail," I
said. "Let's wait and see if he's got the mail."

We hurried down, Kate humming, "Somewhere the sun is
shining," solely, I believe, because she knew it aggravated
me. At any other time I should probably have thrown a pillow
at her, but just now I was too eager to see if Jim Nash had
brought any mail.

I had come from Ontario, the first of September, to visit Uncle Kenneth Morrison's family. I had been looking forward to the trip for several years. My cousin Kate and I had always corresponded since they had "gone west" ten years before; and Kate, who revelled in the western life, had sung the praises of her adopted land rapturously and constantly. It was quite a joke on her that, when I did finally come to visit her, I should have struck the wettest autumn ever recorded in the history of the west. A wet September in Saskatchewan is no joke, however. The country was almost "flooded out." The trails soon became nearly impassable. All our plans for drives and picnics and inter-neighbour visiting – at that time a neighbour meant a man who lived at least six miles away – had to be given up. Yet I was not lonesome, and I enjoyed my visit in spite of everything. Kate was a host in herself. She was twenty-eight years old – eight years my senior – but the difference in our ages had never been any barrier to our friendship. She was a jolly, companionable, philosophical soul, with a jest for every situation, and a merry solution for every perplexity. The only fault I had to find with her was her tendency to make parodies. Kate's parodies were perfectly awful and always got on my nerves.

She was dreadfully ashamed of the way the Saskatchewan weather was behaving after all her boasting. She was thin at the best of times, but now she grew positively scraggy with the worry of it. I am afraid I took an unholy delight in teasing her, and abused the western weather even more than was necessary.

Jim Nash – the lank youth who was hired to look after the place during Uncle Kenneth's absence on a prolonged threshing expedition – had brought some mail. Kate's share was a letter, postmarked Bothwell, a rising little town about one hundred and twenty miles from Arrow Creek. Kate had several friends there, and one of our plans had been to visit Bothwell and spend a week with them. We had meant to drive, of course, since there was no other way of getting there, and equally of course the plan had been abandoned because of the wet weather.

"Mother," exclaimed Kate, "Mary Taylor is going to be married in a fortnight's time! She wants Phil and me to go up to Bothwell for the wedding."

"What a pity you can't go," remarked Aunt Jennie placidly. Aunt Jennie was always a placid little soul, with a most enviable knack of taking everything easy. Nothing ever worried her greatly, and when she had decided that a thing was inevitable it did not worry her at all.

"But I am going," cried Kate. "I will go – I must go. I positively cannot let Mary Taylor – my own beloved Molly – go and perpetrate matrimony without my being on hand to see it. Yes, I'm going – and if Phil has a spark of the old Blair pioneer spirit in her, she'll go too."

"Of course I'll go if you go," I said.

Aunt Jennie did not think we were in earnest, so she merely laughed at first, and said, "How do you propose to go? Fly – or swim?"

"We'll drive, as usual," said Kate calmly. "I'd feel more at home in that way of locomotion. We'll borrow Jim Nash's father's democrat, and take the ponies. We'll put on old clothes, raincoats, rubber caps and boots, and we'll start tomorrow. In an ordinary time we could easily do it in six days or less, but this fall we'll probably need ten or twelve."

"You don't really mean to go, Kate!" said Aunt Jennie, beginning to perceive that Kate did mean it.

"I do," said Kate, in a convincing tone.

Aunt Jennie felt a little worried – as much as she could feel worried over anything – and she tried her best to dissuade Kate, although she plainly did not have much hope of doing so, having had enough experience with her determined daughter to realize that when Kate said she was going to do a thing she did it. It was rather funny to listen to the ensuing dialogue.

"Kate, you can't do it. It's a crazy idea! The road is one hundred and twenty miles long."

"I've driven it twice, Mother."

"Yes, but not in such a wet year. The trail is impassable in places."

"Oh, there are always plenty of dry spots to be found if you only look hard for them."

"But you don't know where to look for them, and goodness knows what you'll get into while you are looking."

"We'll call at the M.P. barracks and get an Indian to guide us. Indians always know the dry spots."

"The stage driver has decided not to make another trip till the October frosts set in."

"But he always has such a heavy load. It will be quite different with us, you must remember. We'll travel light – just our provisions and a valise containing our wedding garments."

"What will you do if you get mired twenty miles from a human being?"

"But we won't. I'm a good driver and I haven't nerves – but I have nerve. Besides, you forget that we'll have an Indian guide with us."

"There was a company of Hudson Bay freighters ambushed and killed along that very trail by Blackfoot Indians in 1839," said Aunt Jennie dolefully.

"Fifty years ago! Their ghosts must have ceased to haunt it by this time," said Kate flippantly.

"Well, you'll get wet through and catch your deaths of cold," protested Aunt Jennie.

"No fear of it. We'll be cased in rubber. And we'll borrow a good tight tent from the M.P.s. Besides, I'm sure it's not going to rain much more. I know the signs."

"At least wait for a day or two until you're sure that it has cleared up," implored Aunt Jennie.

"Which being interpreted means, 'Wait for a day or two, because then your father may be home and he'll squelch your mad expedition,'" said Kate, with a sly glance at me. "No, no, my mother, your wiles are in vain. We'll hit the trail tomorrow at sunrise. So just be good, darling, and help us pack up some provisions. I'll send Jim for his father's democrat."

Aunt Jennie resigned herself to the inevitable and betook herself to the pantry with the air of a woman who washes her hands of the consequences. I flew upstairs to pack some finery. I was wild with delight over the proposed outing. I did not realize what it actually meant, and I had perfect confidence in Kate, who was an expert driver, an experienced camper out, and an excellent manager. If I could have seen what was ahead of us I would certainly not have been quite so jubilant and reckless, but I would have gone all the same. I would not miss the laughter-provoking memories of that trip out of my life for anything. I have always been glad I went.

WE LEFT AT SUNRISE the next morning; there was a sunrise that morning, for a wonder. The sun came up in a pinky-saffron sky and promised us a fine day. Aunt Jennie bade us goodbye and, estimable woman that she was, did not trouble us with advice or forebodings.

Mr. Nash had sent over his "democrat," a light wagon with springs; and Kate's "shaganappies," Tom and Jerry – native ponies, the toughest horse flesh to be found in the world – were hitched to it. Kate and I were properly accoutred for our trip and looked – but I try to forget how we looked! The memory is not flattering.

We drove off in the gayest of spirits. Our difficulties began at the start, for we had to drive a mile before we could find a place to ford the creek. Beyond that, however, we had a passable trail for three miles to the little outpost of the Mounted

Police, where five or six men were stationed on detachment duty.

"Sergeant Baker is a friend of mine," said Kate. "He'll be only too glad to lend me all we require."

The sergeant was a friend of Kate's, but he looked at her as if he thought she was crazy when she told him where we were going.

"You'd better take a canoe instead of a team," he said sarcastically. "I've a good notion to arrest you both as horse thieves and prevent you from going on such a mad expedition."

"You know nothing short of arrest would stop me," said Kate, nodding at him with laughing eyes, "and you really won't go to such an extreme, I know. So please be nice, even if it comes hard, and lend us some things. I've come a-borrying."

"I won't lend you a thing," declared the sergeant. "I won't aid and abet you in any such freak as this. Go home now, like a good girl."

"I'm not going home," said Kate. "I'm not a 'good girl' – I'm a wicked old maid, and I'm going to Bothwell. If you won't lend us a tent we'll go without – and sleep in the open – and our deaths will lie forever at your door. I'll come back and haunt you, if you don't lend me a tent. I'll camp on your very threshold and you won't be able to go out of your door without falling over my spook."

"I've more fear of being accountable for your death if I do let you go," said Sergeant Baker dubiously. "However, I see that nothing but physical force will prevent you. What do you want?"

"I want," said Kate, "a cavalry tent, a sheet-iron camp stove, and a good Indian guide – old Peter Crow for choice. He's such a respectable-looking old fellow, and his wife often works for us."

The sergeant gave us the tent and stove, and sent a man

down to the Reserve for Peter Crow. Moreover, he vindicated his title of friend by making us take a dozen prairie chickens and a large ham – besides any quantity of advice. We didn't want the advice but we hugely welcomed the ham. Presently our guide appeared – quite a spruce old Indian, as Indians go. I had never been able to shake off my childhood conviction that an Indian was a fearsome creature, hopelessly addicted to scalping knives and tomahawks, and I secretly felt quite horrified at the idea of two defenceless females starting out on a lonely prairie trail with an Indian for guide. Even old Peter Crow's meek appearance did not quite reassure me; but I kept my qualms to myself, for I knew Kate would only laugh at me.

It was ten when we finally got away from the M.P. outpost. Sergeant Baker bade us goodbye in a tone which seemed to intimate that he never expected to see either of us again. What with his dismal predictions and my secret horror of Indians, I was beginning to feel anything but jubilant over our expedition. Kate, however, was as blithe and buoyant as usual. She knew no fear, being one of those enviable folk who can because they think they can. One hundred and twenty miles of half-flooded prairie trail – camping out at night in the solitude of the Great Lone Land – rain – muskegs – Indian guides – nothing had any terror for my dauntless cousin.

For the next three hours, however, we got on beautifully. The trail was fair, though somewhat greasy; the sun shone, though with a somewhat watery gleam, through the mists; and Peter Crow, coiled up on the folded tent behind the seat, slept soundly and snored mellifluously. That snore reassured me greatly. I had never thought of Indians as snoring. Surely one who did couldn't be dreaded greatly.

We stopped at one o'clock and had a cold lunch, sitting in our wagon, while Peter Crow wakened up and watered the ponies. We did not get on so well in the afternoon. The trail descended into low-lying ground where travelling was very difficult. I had to admit old Peter Crow was quite invaluable. He knew, as Kate had foretold, "all the dry spots" – that is to say, spots less wet than others. But, even so, we had to make so many detours that by sunset we were little more than six miles distant from our noon halting place.

"We'd better set camp now, before it gets any darker," said Kate. "There's a capital spot over there, by that bluff of dead poplar. The ground seems pretty dry too. Peter, cut us a set of tent poles and kindle a fire."

"Want my dollar first," said old Peter stolidly.

We had agreed to pay him a dollar a day for the trip, but none of the money was to be paid until we got to Bothwell. Kate told him this. But all the reply she got was a stolid, "Want dollar. No make fire without dollar."

We were getting cold and it was getting dark, so finally Kate, under the law of necessity, paid him his dollar. Then he carried out our orders at his own sweet leisure. In course of time he got a fire lighted, and while we cooked supper he set up the tent and prepared our beds, by cutting piles of brush and covering them with rugs.

Kate and I had a hilarious time cooking that supper. It was my first experience of camping out and, as I had become pretty well convinced that Peter Crow was not the typical Indian of old romance, I enjoyed it all hugely. But we were both very tired, and as soon as we had finished eating we betook ourselves to our tent and found our brush beds much more comfortable than I had expected. Old Peter coiled up on his blanket outside by the fire, and the great silence of a windless prairie enwrapped us. In a few minutes we were sound asleep and never wakened until seven o'clock.

WHEN WE AROSE and lifted the flap of the tent we saw a peculiar sight. The little elevation on which we had pitched our camp seemed to be an island in a vast sea of white mist, dotted here and there with other islands. On every hand to the far horizon stretched that strange, phantasmal ocean, and a hazy sun looked over the shifting billows. I had never seen a western mist before and I thought it extremely beautiful; but Kate, to whom it was no novelty, was more cumbered with breakfast cares.

"I'm ravenous," she said, as she bustled about among our stores. "Camping out always does give one such an appetite. Aren't you hungry, Phil?"

"Comfortably so," I admitted. "But where are our ponies? And where is Peter Crow?"

"Probably the ponies have strayed away looking for pea vines. They love and adore pea vines," said Kate, stirring up the fire from under its blanket of grey ashes. "And Peter Crow has gone to look for them, good old fellow. When you do get a conscientious Indian there is no better guide in the world, but they are rare. Now, Philippa-girl, just pry out the sergeant's ham and shave a few slices off it for our breakfast. Some savoury fried ham always goes well on the prairie."

I went for the ham but could not find it. A thorough search among our effects revealed it not.

"Kate, I can't find the ham," I called out. "It must have fallen out somewhere on the trail."

Kate ceased wrestling with the fire and came to help in the search for the missing delicacy.

"It couldn't have fallen out," she said incredulously. "That is impossible. The tent was fastened securely over everything. Nothing could have jolted out."

"Well, then, where is the ham?" I said.

That question was unanswerable, as Kate discovered after another thorough search. The ham was gone – that much was certain.

"I believe Peter Crow has levanted with the ham," I said decidedly.

"I don't believe Peter Crow could be so dishonest," said

Kate rather shortly. "His wife has worked for us for years, and she's as honest as the sunlight."

"Honesty isn't catching," I remarked, but I said nothing more just then, for Kate's black eyes were snapping.

"Anyway, we can't have ham for breakfast," she said, twitching out the frying pan rather viciously. "We'll have to put up with canned chicken – if the cans haven't disappeared too."

They hadn't, and we soon produced a very tolerable breakfast. But neither of us had much appetite.

"Do you suppose Peter Crow has taken the horses as well as the ham?" I asked.

"No," gloomily responded Kate, who had evidently been compelled by the logic of hard facts to believe in Peter's guilt, "he would hardly dare to do that, because he couldn't dispose of them without being found out. They've probably strayed away on their own account when Peter decamped. As soon as this mist lifts I'll have a look for them. They can't have gone far."

We were spared this trouble, however, for when we were washing up the dishes the ponies returned of their own accord. Kate caught them and harnessed them.

"Are we going on?" I asked mildly.

"Of course we're going on," said Kate, her good humour entirely restored. "Do you suppose I'm going to be turned from my purpose by the defection of a miserable old Indian? Oh, wait till he comes round in the winter, begging."

"Will he come?" I asked.

"Will he? Yes, my dear, he will – with a smooth, plausible story to account for his desertion and a bland denial of ever having seen our ham. I shall know how to deal with him then, the old scamp."

"When you do get a conscientious Indian there's no better guide in the world, but they are rare," I remarked with a far-away look.

Kate laughed.

"Don't rub it in, Phil. Come, help me to break camp. We'll have to work harder and hustle for ourselves, that's all."

"But is it safe to go on without a guide?" I inquired dubiously. I hadn't felt very safe with Peter Crow, but I felt still more unsafe without him.

"Safe! Of course, it's safe – perfectly safe. I know the trail, and we'll just have to drive around the wet places. It would have been easier with Peter, and we'd have had less work to do, but we'll get along well enough without him. I don't think I'd have bothered with him at all, only I wanted to set Mother's mind at rest. She'll never know he isn't with us till the trip is over, so that is all right. We're going to have a glorious day. But, oh, for our lost ham! 'The Ham That Was Never Eaten.' There's a subject for a poem, Phil. You write one when we get back to civilization. Methinks I can sniff the savoury odour of that lost ham on all the prairie breezes."

> "Of all sad words of tongue or pen,
> The saddest are these – it might have been,"

I quoted, beginning to wash the dishes.

> "Saw ye my wee ham, saw ye my ain ham,
>   Saw ye my pork ham down on yon lea?
> Crossed it the prairie last night in the darkness
>   Borne by an old and unprincipled Cree?"

sang Kate, loosening the tent ropes. Altogether, we got a great deal more fun out of that ham than if we had eaten it.

As Kate had predicted, the day was glorious. The mists rolled away and the sun shone brightly. We drove all day without stopping, save for dinner – when the lost ham figured largely in our conversation – of course. We said so many witty things about it – at least, we thought them witty – that we laughed continuously through the whole meal, which we ate with prodigious appetite.

But with all our driving we were not getting on very fast. The country was exceedingly swampy and we had to make innumerable detours.

"'The longest way round is the shortest way to Bothwell,'" said Kate, when we drove five miles out of our way to avoid a muskeg. By evening we had driven fully twenty-five miles, but we were only ten miles nearer Bothwell than when we had broken camp in the morning.

"We'll have to camp soon," sighed Kate. "I believe around this bluff will be a good place. Oh, Phil, I'm tired – dead tired! My very thoughts are tired. I can't even think anything funny about the ham. And yet we've got to set up the tent ourselves, and attend to the horses; and we'll have to scrape some of the mud off this beautiful vehicle."

"We can leave that till the morning," I suggested.

"No, it will be too hard and dry then. Here we are – and here are two tepees of Indians also!"

There they were, right around the bluff. The inmates were standing in a group before them, looking at us as composedly as if we were not at all an unusual sight.

"I'm going to stay here anyhow," said Kate doggedly.

"Oh, don't," I said in alarm. "They're such a villainous-looking lot – so dirty – and they've got so little clothing on. I wouldn't sleep a wink near them. Look at that awful old squaw with only one eye. They'd steal everything we've got left, Kate. Remember the ham – oh, pray remember the fate of our beautiful ham."

"I shall never forget that ham," said Kate wearily, "but, Phil, we can't drive far enough to be out of their reach if they really want to steal our provisions. But I don't believe they will. I believe they have plenty of food – Indians in tepees mostly have. The men hunt, you know. Their looks are proba-bly the worst of them. Anyhow, you can't judge Indians by appearances. Peter Crow looked respectable – and he was a whited sepulchre. Now, these Indians look as bad as Indians can look – so they may turn out to be angels in disguise."

"Very much disguised, certainly," I acquiesced satirically. "They seem to me to belong to the class of a neighbour of ours down east. Her family is always in rags, because she says, 'a hole is an accident, a patch is a disgrace.' Set camp here if you like, Kate. But I'll not sleep a wink with such neighbours."

I cheerfully ate my words later on. Never were appearances more deceptive than in the case of those Stoneys. There is an old saying that many a kind heart beats behind a ragged coat. The Indians had no coats for their hearts to beat behind – nothing but shirts – some of them hadn't even shirts! But the shirts were certainly ragged enough, and their hearts were kind.

Those Indians were gentlemen. They came forward and unhitched our horses, fed, and watered them; they pitched our tent, and built us a fire, and cut brush for our beds. Kate and I had simply nothing to do except sit on our rugs and tell them what we wanted done. They would have cooked our supper for us if we had allowed it. But, tired as we were, we drew the line at that. Their hearts were pure gold, but their hands! No, Kate and I dragged ourselves up and cooked our own suppers. And while we ate it, those Indians fell to and cleaned all the mud off our democrat for us. To crown all – it is almost unbelievable but it is true, I solemnly avow – they wouldn't take a cent of payment for it all, urge them as we might and did.

"Well," said Kate, as we curled up on our brush beds that night, "there certainly is a special Providence for unprotected females. I'd forgive Peter Crow for deserting us for the sake of those Indians, if he hadn't stolen our lovely ham into the bargain. That was altogether unpardonable."

In the morning the Indians broke camp for us and harnessed our shaganappies. We drove off, waving our hands to them, the delightful creatures. We never saw any of them again. I fear their kind is scarce, but as long as I live I shall remember those Stoneys with gratitude.

We got on fairly well that third day, and made about fifteen miles before dinner time. We ate three of the sergeant's prairie chickens for dinner, and enjoyed them.

"But only think how delicious the ham would have been," said Kate.

Our real troubles began that afternoon. We had not been driving long when the trail swooped down suddenly into a broad depression – a swamp, so full of mud-holes that there didn't seem to be anything but mud-holes. We pulled through six of them – but in the seventh we stuck, hard and fast. Pull as our ponies could and did, they could not pull us out.

"What are we to do?" I said, becoming horribly frightened all at once. It seemed to me that our predicament was a dreadful one.

"Keep cool," said Kate. She calmly took off her shoes and stockings, tucked up her skirt, and waded to the horses' heads.

"Can't I do anything?" I implored.

"Yes, take the whip and spare it not," said Kate. "I'll encourage them here with sundry tugs and inspiriting words. You urge them behind with a good lambasting."

Accordingly we encouraged and urged, tugged and lambasted, with a right good will, but all to no effect. Our ponies did their best, but they could not pull the democrat out of that slough.

"Oh, what –" I began, and then I stopped. I resolved that I would not ask that question again in that tone in that scrape. I would be cheerful and courageous like Kate – splendid Kate!

"I shall have to unhitch them, tie one of them to that stump, and ride off on the other for help," said Kate.

"Where to?" I asked.

"Till I find it," grinned Kate, who seemed to think the

whole disaster a capital joke. "I may have to go clean back to the tepees – and further. For that matter, I don't believe there were any tepees. Those Indians were too good to be true – they were phantoms of delight – such stuff as dreams are made of. But even if they were real they won't be there now – they'll have folded their tents like the Arabs and as silently stolen away. But I'll find help somewhere."

"I can't stay here alone. You may be gone for hours," I cried, forgetting all my resolutions of courage and cheerfulness in an access of panic.

"Then ride the other pony and come with me," suggested Kate.

"I can't ride bareback," I moaned.

"Then you'll have to stay here," said Kate decidedly. "There's nothing to hurt you, Phil. Sit in the wagon and keep dry. Eat something if you get hungry. I may not be very long."

I realized that there was nothing else to do; and, rather ashamed of my panic, I resigned myself to the inevitable and saw Kate off with a smile of encouragement. Then I waited. I was tired and frightened – horribly frightened. I sat there and imagined scores of gruesome possibilities. It was no use telling myself to be brave. I couldn't be brave. I never was in such a blue funk before or since. Suppose Kate got lost – suppose she couldn't find me again – suppose something happened to her – suppose she couldn't get help – suppose it came on night and I there all alone – suppose Indians – not gentlemanly Stoneys or even Peter Crows, but genuine, old-fashioned Indians – should come along – suppose it began to pour rain!

It did begin to rain, the only one of my suppositions which came true. I hoisted an umbrella and sat there grimly, in that horseless wagon in the mud-hole.

MANY A TIME SINCE have I laughed over the memory of the appearance I must have presented sitting in that mud-hole, but there was nothing in the least funny about it at the time.

The worst feature of it all was the uncertainty. I could have waited patiently enough and conquered my fears if I had known that Kate would find help and return within a reasonable time – at least before dark. But everything was doubtful. I was not composed of the stuff out of which heroines are fashioned and I devoutly wished we had never left Arrow Creek.

Shouts – calls – laughter – Kate's dear voice in an encouraging cry from the hill behind me!

"Halloo, honey! Hold the fort a few minutes longer. Here we are. Bless her, hasn't she been a brick to stay here all alone like this – and a tenderfoot at that?"

I could have cried with joy. But I saw that there were men with Kate – two men – white men – and I laughed instead. I had not been brave – I had been an arrant little coward, but I vowed that nobody, not even Kate, should suspect it. Later on Kate told me how she had fared in her search for assistance.

"When I left you, Phil, I felt much more anxious than I wanted to let you see. I had no idea where to go. I knew there were no houses along our trail and I might have to go clean back to the tepees – fifteen miles bareback. I didn't dare try any other trail, for I knew nothing of them and wasn't sure that there were even tepees on them. But when I had gone about six miles I saw a welcome sight – nothing less than a spiral of blue, homely-looking smoke curling up from the prairie far off to my right. I decided to turn off and investigate. I rode two miles and finally I came to a little log shack. There was a bee-yew-tiful big horse in a corral close by. My heart jumped with joy. But suppose the inmates of the shack were half-breeds! You can't realize how relieved I felt when the door opened and two white men came out. In a few minutes everything was explained. They knew who I was and what I wanted, and I knew that they were Mr. Lonsdale and Mr. Hopkins, owners of a big ranch over by Deer Run. They were 'shacking out' to put up some hay and Mrs. Hopkins was keeping house for them. She wanted me to stop and have a cup of tea right off, but I thought of you, Phil, and declined. As soon as they heard of our predicament those lovely men got their two biggest horses and came right with me."

It was not long before our democrat was on solid ground once more, and then our rescuers insisted that we go back to the shack with them for the night. Accordingly we drove back to the shack, attended by our two gallant deliverers on white horses. Mrs. Hopkins was waiting for us, a trim, dark-haired little lady in a very pretty gown, which she had donned in our honour. Kate and I felt like perfect tramps beside her in our muddy old raiment, with our hair dressed by dead reckoning – for we had not included a mirror in our baggage. There was a mirror in the shack, however – small but good – and we quickly made ourselves tidy at least, and Kate even went to the length of curling her bangs – bangs were in style then and Kate had long, thick ones – using the stem of a broken pipe of Mr. Hopkins's for a curler. I was so tired that my vanity was completely crushed out – for the time being – and I simply pinned my bangs back. Later on, when I discovered that Mr. Lonsdale was really the younger son of an English earl, I wished I had curled them, but it was too late then.

He didn't look in the least like a scion of aristocracy. He wore a cowboy rig and had a scrubby beard of a week's growth. But he was very jolly and played the violin beautifully. After tea – and a lovely tea it was, although, as Kate remarked to me later, there was no ham – we had an impromptu concert. Mr. Lonsdale played the violin; Mrs. Hopkins, who sang, was a graduate of a musical conservatory; Mr. Hopkins gave a comic recitation and did a Cree war-dance; Kate gave a spir-ited account of our adventures since leaving home and mother; and I described – with trimmings – how I felt sitting alone in the democrat in a mud-hole, in a pouring rain on a vast prairie.

Mrs. Hopkins, Kate, and I slept in the one bed the shack boasted, screened off from public view by a calico curtain. Mr. Lonsdale reposed in his accustomed bunk by the stove, but poor Mr. Hopkins had to sleep on the floor. He must have been glad Kate and I stayed only one night.

THE FOURTH MORNING found us blithely hitting the trail in renewed confidence and spirits. We parted from our kind friends in the shack with mutual regret. Mr. Hopkins gave us a haunch of jumping deer and Mrs. Hopkins gave us a box of home-made cookies. Mr. Lonsdale at first thought he couldn't give us anything, for he said all he had with him was his pipe and his fiddle; but later on he said he felt so badly to see us go without any token of his good will that he felt constrained to ask us to accept a piece of rope that he had tied his outfit together with.

The fourth day we got on so nicely that it was quite monotonous. The sun shone, the chinook blew, our ponies trotted over the trail gallantly. Kate and I sang, told stories, and laughed immoderately over everything. Even a poor joke seems to have a subtle flavour on the prairie. For the first time I began to think Saskatchewan beautiful, with those far-reaching parklike meadows dotted with the white-stemmed poplars, the distant bluffs bannered with the airiest of purple hazes, and the little blue lakes that sparkled and shimmered in the sunlight on every hand.

The only thing approaching an adventure that day happened in the afternoon when we reached a creek which had to be crossed.

"We must investigate," said Kate decidedly. "It would never do to risk getting mired here, for this country is unsettled and we must be twenty miles from another human being."

Kate again removed her shoes and stockings and puddled

about that creek until she found a safe fording place. I am afraid I must admit that I laughed most heartlessly at the spectacle she presented while so employed.

"Oh, for a camera, Kate!" I said, between spasms.

Kate grinned. "I don't care what I look like," she said, "but I feel wretchedly unpleasant. This water is simply swarming with wigglers."

"Goodness, what are they?" I exclaimed.

"Oh, they're tiny little things like leeches," responded Kate. "I believe they develop into mosquitoes later on, bad 'cess to them. What Mr. Nash would call my pedal extremities are simply being devoured by the brutes. Ugh! I believe the bottom of this creek is all soft mud. We may have to drive – no, as I'm a living, wiggler-haunted human being, here's firm bottom. Hurrah, Phil, we're all right!"

In a few minutes we were past the creek and bowling merrily on our way. We had a beautiful camping ground that night – a fairylike little slope of white poplars with a blue lake at its foot. When the sun went down a milk-white mist hung over the prairie, with a young moon kissing it. We boiled some slices of our jumping deer and ate them in the open around a cheery camp-fire. Then we sought our humble couches, where we slept the sleep of just people who had been driving over the prairie all day. Once in the night I wakened. It was very dark. The unearthly stillness of a great prairie was all around me. In that vast silence Kate's soft breathing at my side seemed an intrusion of sound where no sound should be.

"Philippa Blair, can you believe it's yourself?" I said mentally. "Here you are, lying on a brush bed on a western prairie in the middle of the night, at least twenty miles from any human being except another frail creature of your own sex. Yet you're not even frightened. You are very comfy and composed, and you're going right to sleep again."

And right to sleep again I went.

OUR FIFTH DAY began ominously. We had made an early start and had driven about six miles when the calamity occurred. Kate turned a corner too sharply, to avoid a big boulder; there was a heart-breaking sound.

"The tongue of the wagon is broken," cried Kate in dismay. All too surely it was. We looked at each other blankly.

"What can we do?" I said.

"I'm sure I don't know," said Kate helplessly. When Kate felt helpless I thought things must be desperate indeed. We got out and investigated the damage.

"It's not a clean break," said Kate. "It's a long, slanting break. If we had a piece of rope I believe I could fix it."

"Mr. Lonsdale's piece of rope!" I cried.

"The very thing," said Kate, brightening up.

The rope was found and we set to work. With the aid of some willow withes and that providential rope we contrived to splice the tongue together in some shape.

Although the trail was good we made only twelve miles the rest of the day, so slowly did we have to drive. Besides, we were continually expecting that tongue to give way again, and the strain was bad for our nerves. When we came at sunset to the junction of the Black River trail with ours, Kate resolutely turned the shaganappies down it.

"We'll go and spend the night with the Brewsters," she said. "They live only ten miles down this trail. I went to school in Regina with Hannah Brewster, and though I haven't seen her for ten years I know she'll be glad to see us. She's a lovely person, and her husband is a very nice man. I visited them once after they were married."

We soon arrived at the Brewster place. It was a trim, whitewashed little log house in a grove of poplars. But all the blinds were down and we discovered the door was locked. Evidently the Brewsters were not at home.

"Never mind," said Kate cheerfully, "we'll light a fire

outside and cook our supper and then we'll spend the night in the barn. A bed of prairie hay will be just the thing."

But the barn was locked too. It was now dark and our plight was rather desperate.

"I'm going to get into the house if I have to break a window," said Kate resolutely. "Hannah would want us to do that. She'd never get over it, if she heard we came to her house and couldn't get in."

Fortunately we did not have to go to the length of breaking into Hannah's house. The kitchen window went up quite easily. We turned the shaganappies loose to forage for themselves, grass and water being abundant. Then we climbed in at the window, lighted our lantern, and found ourselves in a very snug little kitchen. Opening off it on one side was a trim, nicely furnished parlour and on the other a well-stocked pantry.

"We'll light the fire in the stove in a jiffy and have a real good supper," said Kate exultantly. "Here's cold roast beef – and preserves and cookies and cheese and butter."

Before long we had supper ready and we did full justice to the absent Hannah's excellent cheer. After all, it was quite nice to sit down once more to a well-appointed table and eat in civilized fashion.

Then we washed up all the dishes and made everything snug and tidy. I shall never be sufficiently thankful that we did so.

Kate piloted me upstairs to the spare room.

"This is fixed up much nicer than it was when I was here before," she said, looking around. "Of course, Hannah and Ted were just starting out then and they had to be economical. They must have prospered, to be able to afford such furniture as this. Well, turn in, Phil. Won't it be rather jolly to sleep between sheets once more?"

We slept long and soundly until half-past eight the next

morning; and dear knows if we would have wakened then of our own accord. But I heard somebody saying in a very harsh, gruff voice, "Here, you two, wake up! I want to know what this means."

We two did wake up, promptly and effectually. I never wakened up so thoroughly in my life before. Standing in our room were three people, one of them a man. He was a big, grey-haired man with a bushy black beard and an angry scowl. Beside him was a woman – a tall, thin, angular personage with red hair and an indescribable bonnet. She looked even crosser and more amazed than the man, if that were possible. In the background was another woman – a tiny old lady who must have been at least eighty. She was, in spite of her tininess, a very striking-looking personage; she was dressed all in black, and had snow-white hair, a dead-white face, and snapping, vivid, coal-black eyes. She looked as amazed as the other two, but she didn't look cross.

I knew something must be wrong – fearfully wrong – but I didn't know what. Even in my confusion, I found time to think that if that disagreeable-looking red-haired woman was Hannah Brewster, Kate must have had a queer taste in school friends. Then the man said, more gruffly than ever, "Come now. Who are you and what business have you here?"

Kate raised herself on one elbow. She looked very wild. I heard the old black-and-white lady in the background chuckle to herself.

"Isn't this Theodore Brewster's place?" gasped Kate.

"No," said the big woman, speaking for the first time. "This place belongs to us. We bought it from the Brewsters in the spring. They moved over to Black River Forks. Our name is Chapman."

Poor Kate fell back on the pillow, quite overcome. "I – I beg your pardon," she said. "I – I thought the Brewsters lived here. Mrs. Brewster is a friend of mine. My cousin and I are on our way to Bothwell and we called here to spend the night with Hannah. When we found everyone away we just came in and made ourselves at home."

"A likely story," said the red woman.

"We weren't born yesterday," said the man.

Madam Black-and-White didn't say anything, but when the other two had made their pretty speeches she doubled up in a silent convulsion of mirth, shaking her head from side to side and beating the air with her hands.

If they had been nice to us, Kate would probably have gone on feeling confused and ashamed. But when they were so disagreeable she quickly regained her self-possession. She sat up again and said in her haughtiest voice, "I do not know when you were born, or where, but it must have been somewhere where very peculiar manners were taught. If you will have the decency to leave our room – this room – until we can get up and dress we will not transgress upon your hospitality" (Kate put a most satirical emphasis on that word) "any longer. And we shall pay you amply for the food we have eaten and the night's lodging we have taken."

The black-and-white apparition went through the motion of clapping her hands, but not a sound did she make. Whether he was cowed by Kate's tone, or appeased by the prospect of payment, I know not, but Mr. Chapman spoke more civilly. "Well, that's fair. If you pay up it's all right."

"They shall do no such thing as pay you," said Madam Black-and-White in a surprisingly clear, resolute, authoritative voice. "If you haven't any shame for yourself, Robert Chapman, you've got a mother-in-law who can be ashamed for you. No strangers shall be charged for food or lodging in any house where Mrs. Matilda Pitman lives. Remember that I've come down in the world, but I haven't forgot all decency for all that. I knew you was a skinflint when Amelia married you and you've made her as bad as yourself. But I'm boss here yet. Here, you, Robert Chapman, take yourself out of here and let those girls get dressed. And you, Amelia, go downstairs and cook a breakfast for them."

I never, in all my life, saw anything like the abject meekness with which those two big people obeyed that mite. They went, and stood not upon the order of their going. As the door closed behind them, Mrs. Matilda Pitman laughed silently, and rocked from side to side in her merriment.

"Ain't it funny?" she said. "I mostly lets them run the length of their tether but sometimes I has to pull them up, and then I does it with a jerk. Now, you can take your time about dressing, my dears, and I'll go down and keep them in order, the mean scalawags."

When we descended the stairs we found a smoking-hot breakfast on the table. Mr. Chapman was nowhere to be seen, and Mrs. Chapman was cutting bread with a sulky air. Mrs. Matilda Pitman was sitting in an armchair, knitting. She still wore her bonnet and her triumphant expression. "Set right in, dears, and make a good breakfast," she said.

"We are not hungry," said Kate, almost pleadingly. "I don't think we can eat anything. And it's time we were on the trail. Please excuse us and let us go on."

Mrs. Matilda Pitman shook a knitting needle playfully at Kate. "Sit down and take your breakfast," she commanded. "Mrs. Matilda Pitman commands you. Everybody obeys Mrs. Matilda Pitman – even Robert and Amelia. You must obey her too."

We did obey her. We sat down and, such was the influence of her mesmeric eyes, we ate a tolerable breakfast. The obedient Amelia never spoke; Mrs. Matilda Pitman did not speak either, but she knitted furiously and chuckled. When we had finished Mrs. Matilda Pitman rolled up her knitting. "Now, you can go if you want to," she said, "but you don't have to go. You can stay here as long as you like, and I'll make them cook your meals for you."

I never saw Kate so thoroughly cowed.

"Thank you," she said faintly. "You are very kind, but we must go."

"Well, then," said Mrs. Matilda Pitman, throwing open the door, "your team is ready for you. I made Robert catch your ponies and harness them. And I made him fix that broken tongue properly. I enjoy making Robert do things. It's almost the only sport I have left. I'm eighty and most things have lost their flavour, except bossing Robert."

Our democrat and ponies were outside the door, but Robert was nowhere to be seen; in fact, we never saw him again.

"I do wish," said Kate, plucking up what little spirit she had left, "that you would let us – ah – uh" – Kate quailed before Mrs. Matilda Pitman's eye – "recompense you for our entertainment."

"Mrs. Matilda Pitman said before – and meant it – that she doesn't take pay for entertaining strangers, nor let other people where she lives do it, much as their meanness would like to do it."

We got away. The sulky Amelia had vanished, and there was nobody to see us off except Mrs. Matilda Pitman.

"Don't forget to call the next time you come this way," she said cheerfully, waving her knitting at us. "I hope you'll get safe to Bothwell. If I was ten years younger I vow I'd pack a grip and go along with you. I like your spunk. Most of the girls nowadays is such timid, skeery critters. When I was a girl I wasn't afraid of nothing or nobody."

We said and did nothing until we had driven out of sight and earshot. Then Kate laid down the reins and laughed until the tears came.

"Oh, Phil, Phil, will you ever forget this adventure?" she gasped.

"I shall never forget Mrs. Matilda Pitman," I said emphatically.

We had no further adventures that day. Robert Chapman

had fixed the tongue so well – probably under Mrs. Matilda Pitman's watchful eyes – that we could drive as fast as we liked, and we made good progress. But when we pitched camp that night Kate scanned the sky with an anxious expression. "I don't like the look of it," she said. "I'm afraid we're going to have a bad day tomorrow."

WE HAD. When we awakened in the morning rain was pouring down. This in itself might not have prevented us from travelling, but the state of the trail did. It had been raining the greater part of the night and the trail was little more than a ditch of slimy, greasy, sticky mud.

If we could have stayed in the tent the whole time it would not have been quite so bad. But we had to go out twice to take the ponies to the nearest pond and water them; moreover, we had to collect pea vines for them, which was not an agreeable occupation in a pouring rain. The day was very cold too, but fortunately there was plenty of dead poplar right by our camp. We kept a good fire on in the camp stove and were quite dry and comfortable as long as we stayed inside. Even when we had to go out we did not get very wet, as we were well protected. But it was a long dreary day. Finally when the dark came down and supper was over Kate grew quite desperate. "Let's have a game of checkers," she suggested.

"Where is your checkerboard?" I asked.

"Oh, I'll soon furnish that," said Kate.

She cut out a square of brown paper, in which a biscuit box had been wrapped, and marked squares off on it with a pencil. Then she produced some red and white high-bush cranberries for men. A cranberry split in two was a king.

We played nine games of checkers by the light of our smoky lantern. Our enjoyment of the game was heightened by the fact that it had ceased raining. Nevertheless, when morning came the trail was so drenched that it was impossible to travel on it.

"We must wait till noon," said Kate.

"That trail won't be dry enough to travel on for a week," I said disconsolately.

"My dear, the chinook is blowing up," said Kate. "You don't know how quickly a trail dries in a chinook. It's like magic."

I did not believe a chinook or anything else could dry up that trail by noon sufficiently for us to travel on. But it did. As Kate said, it seemed like magic. By one o'clock we were on our way again, the chinook blowing merrily against our faces. It was a wind that blew straight from the heart of the wilderness and had in it all the potent lure of the wild. The yellow prairie laughed and glistened in the sun.

We made twenty-five miles that afternoon and, as we were again fortunate enough to find a bluff of dead poplar near which to camp, we built a royal camp-fire which sent its flaming light far and wide over the dark prairie.

We were in jubilant spirits. If the next day were fine and nothing dreadful happened to us, we would reach Bothwell before night.

But our ill luck was not yet at an end. The next morning was beautiful. The sun shone warm and bright; the chinook blew balmily and alluringly; the trail stretched before us dry and level. But we sat moodily before our tent, not even having sufficient heart to play checkers. Tom had gone lame – so lame that there was no use in thinking of trying to travel with him. Kate could not tell what was the matter.

"There is no injury that I can see," she said. "He must have sprained his foot somehow."

Wait we did, with all the patience we could command. But the day was long and wearisome, and at night Tom's foot did not seem a bit better.

We went to bed gloomily, but joy came with the morning. Tom's foot was so much improved that Kate decided we could go on, though we would have to drive slowly.

"There's no chance of making Bothwell today," she said, "but at least we shall be getting a little nearer to it."

"I don't believe there is such a place as Bothwell, or any other town," I said pessimistically. "There's nothing in the world but prairie, and we'll go on driving over it forever, like a couple of female Wandering Jews. It seems years since we left Arrow Creek."

"Well, we've had lots of fun out of it all, you know," said Kate. "Mrs. Matilda Pitman alone was worth it. She will be an amusing memory all our lives. Are you sorry you came?"

"No, I'm not," I concluded, after honest, soul-searching reflection. "No, I'm glad, Kate. But I think we were crazy to attempt it, as Sergeant Baker said. Think of all the might-have-beens."

"Nothing else will happen," said Kate. "I feel in my bones that our troubles are over."

Kate's bones proved true prophets. Nevertheless, that day was a weary one. There was no scenery. We had got into a barren, lakeless, treeless district where the world was one monotonous expanse of grey-brown prairie. We just crawled along. Kate had her hands full driving those ponies. Jerry was in capital fettle and couldn't understand why he mightn't tear ahead at full speed. He was so much disgusted over being compelled to walk that he was very fractious. Poor Tom limped patiently along. But by night his lameness had quite disappeared, and although we were still a good twenty-five miles from Bothwell we could see it quite distinctly far ahead on the level prairie.

"'Tis a sight for sore eyes, isn't it?" said Kate, as we pitched camp.

There is little more to be told. Next day at noon we rattled through the main and only street of Bothwell. Curious sights are frequent in prairie towns, so we did not attract much attention. When we drew up before Mr. Taylor's house Mary Taylor flew out and embraced Kate publicly.

"You darling! I knew you'd get here if anyone could. They telegraphed us you were on the way. You're a brick – two bricks."

"No, I'm not a brick at all, Miss Taylor," I confessed frankly. "I've been an arrant coward and a doubting Thomas and a wet blanket all through the expedition. But Kate is a brick and a genius and an all-round, jolly good fellow."

"Mary," said Kate in a tragic whisper, "have – you – any – ham – in – the – house?"

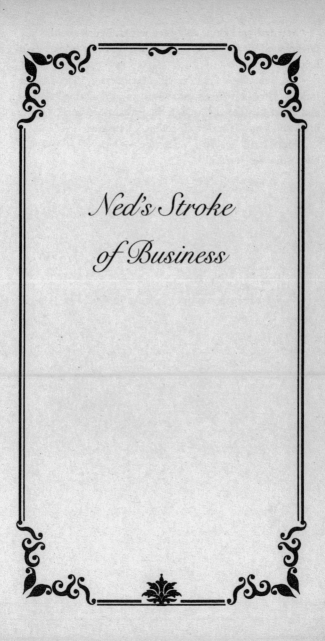

Ned's Stroke
of Business

UMP IN, Ned; I can give you a lift if you're going my way." Mr. Rogers reined up his prancing grey horse, and Ned Allen sprang lightly into the comfortable cutter. The next minute they were flying down the long, glistening road, rosy-white in the sunset splendour. The first snow of the season had come, and the sleighing was, as Ned said, "dandy."

"Going over to Windsor, I suppose," said Mr. Rogers, with a glance at the skates that were hanging over Ned's shoulder.

"Yes, sir; all the Carleton boys are going over tonight. The moon is out, and the ice is good. We have to go in a body, or the Windsor fellows won't leave us alone. There's safety in numbers."

"Pretty hard lines when boys have to go six miles for a skate," commented Mr. Rogers.

"Well, it's that or nothing," laughed Ned. "There isn't a saucerful of ice any nearer, except that small pond in Old Dutcher's field, behind his barn. And you know Old Dutcher won't allow a boy to set foot there. He says they would knock down his fences climbing over them, and like as not set fire to his barn."

"Old Dutcher was always a crank," said Mr. Rogers, "and doubtless will be to the end. By the way, I heard a rumour to the effect that you are soon going to take a course at the business college in Trenton. I hope it's true."

Ned's frank face clouded over. "I'm afraid not, sir. The truth is, I guess Mother can't afford it. Of course, Aunt Ella has very kindly offered to board me free for the term, but fees, books, and so on would require at least fifty dollars. I don't expect to go."

"That's a pity. Can't you earn the necessary money yourself?"

Ned shook his head. "Not much chance for that in Carleton, Mr. Rogers. I've cudgelled my brains for the past month trying to think of some way, but in vain. Well, here is the crossroad, so I must get off. Thank you for the drive, sir."

"Keep on thinking, Ned," advised Mr. Rogers, as the lad jumped out. "Perhaps you'll hit on some plan yet to earn that money, and if you do – well, it will prove that you have good stuff in you."

"I think it would," laughed Ned to himself, as he trudged away. "A quiet little farming village in winter isn't exactly a promising field for financial operations."

At Winterby Corners Ned found a crowd of boys waiting for him, and soon paired off with his chum, Jim Slocum. Jim, as usual, was grumbling because they had to go all the way to Windsor to skate.

"Like as not we'll get into a free fight with the Windsorites when we get there, and be chevied off the ice," he complained.

The rivalry which existed between the Carleton and the Windsor boys was bitter and of long standing.

"We ought to be able to hold our own tonight," said Ned. "There'll be thirty of us there."

"If we could only get Old Dutcher to let us skate on his pond!" said Jim. "It wouldn't hurt his old pond! And the ice is always splendid on it. I'd give a lot if we could only go there."

Ned was silent. A sudden idea had come to him. He wondered if it were feasible. "Anyhow, I'll try it," he said to himself. "I'll interview Old Dutcher tomorrow."

The skating that night was not particularly successful. The small pond at Windsor was crowded, the Windsor boys being out in force and, although no positive disturbance arose, they contrived to make matters unpleasant for the Carletonites, who tramped moodily homeward in no very good humour, most of them declaring that, skating or no skating, they would not go to Windsor again.

The next day Ned Allen went down to see Mr. Dutcher, or Old Dutcher, as he was universally called in Carleton. Ned did not exactly look forward to the interview with pleasure. Old Dutcher was a crank – there was no getting around that fact. He had "good days" occasionally when, for him, he was fairly affable, but they were few and far between, and Ned had no reason to hope that this would be one. Old Dutcher was unmarried, and his widowed sister kept house for him. This poor lady had a decidedly lonely life of it, for Old Dutcher studiously discouraged visitors. His passion for solitude was surpassed only by his eagerness to make and save money. Although he was well-to-do, he would wrangle over a cent, and was the terror of all who had ever had dealings with him.

Fortunately for Ned and his project, this did turn out to be one of Old Dutcher's good days. He had just concluded an advantageous bargain with a Windsor cattle-dealer, and hence he received Ned with what, for Old Dutcher, might be called absolute cordiality. Besides, although Old Dutcher disliked all boys on principle, he disliked Ned less than the rest because the boy had always treated him respectfully and had never played any tricks on him on Hallowe'en or April Fool's Day.

"I've come down to see you on a little matter of business, Mr. Dutcher," said Ned, boldly and promptly. It never did to beat about the bush with Old Dutcher; you had to come straight to the point. "I want to know if you will rent your pond behind the barn to me for a skating-rink."

Old Dutcher's aspect was certainly not encouraging. "No, I won't. You ought to know that. I never allow anyone to skate there. I ain't going to have a parcel of whooping, yelling youngsters tearing over my fences, disturbing my sleep at nights, and like as not setting fire to my barns. No, sir! I ain't going to rent that pond for no skating-rink."

Ned smothered a smile. "Just wait a moment, Mr. Dutcher," he said respectfully. "I want you to hear my proposition before you refuse definitely. First, I'll give you ten dollars for the rent of the pond; then I'll see that there will be no running over your fields and climbing your fences, no lighting of fire or matches about it, and no 'whooping and yelling' at nights. My rink will be open only from two to six in the afternoon and from seven to ten in the evening. During that time I shall always be at the pond to keep everything in order. The skaters will come and go by the lane leading from the barn to the road. I think that if you agree to my proposition, Mr. Dutcher, you will not regret it."

"What's to prevent my running such a rink myself?" asked Old Dutcher gruffly.

"It wouldn't pay you, Mr. Dutcher," answered Ned promptly. "The Carleton boys wouldn't patronize a rink run by you."

Old Dutcher's eyes twinkled. It did not displease him to know that the Carleton boys hated him. In fact, it seemed as if he rather liked it.

"Besides," went on Ned, "you couldn't afford the time. You couldn't be on the pond for eight hours a day and until ten o'clock at night. I can, as I've nothing else to do just now. If I had, I wouldn't have to be trying to make money by a skating-rink."

Old Dutcher scowled. Ten dollars was ten dollars and, as Ned had said, he knew very well that he could not run a rink by himself. "Well," he said, half reluctantly, "I suppose I'll let you go ahead. Only remember I'll hold you responsible if anything happens."

Ned went home in high spirits. By the next day he had placards out in conspicuous places – on the schoolhouse, at the forge, at Mr. Rogers's store, and at Winterby Corners – announcing that he had rented Mr. Dutcher's pond for a skating-rink, and that tickets for the same at twenty-five cents a week for each skater could be had upon application to him.

Ned was not long left in doubt as to the success of his enterprise. It was popular from the start. There were about fifty boys in Carleton and Winterby, and they all patronized the rink freely. At first Ned had some trouble with two or three rowdies, who tried to evade his rules. He was backed up, however, by Old Dutcher's reputation and by the public opinion of the other boys, as well as by his own undoubted muscle, and soon had everything going smoothly. The rink flourished amain, and everybody, even Old Dutcher, was highly pleased.

At the end of the season Ned paid Old Dutcher his ten dollars, and had plenty left to pay for books and tuition at the business college in Trenton. On the eve of his departure Mr. Rogers, who had kept a keen eye on Ned's enterprise, again picked him up on the road.

"So you found a way after all, Ned," he said genially. "I had an idea you would. My bookkeeper will be leaving me about the time you will be through at the college. I will be wanting in his place a young man with a good nose for business, and I rather think that you will be that young man. What do you say?"

"Thank you, sir," stammered Ned, scarcely believing his ears. A position in Mr. Rogers's store meant good salary and promotion. He had never dared to hope for such good fortune. "If you – think I can give satisfaction –"

"You manipulated Old Dutcher, and you've earned enough in a very slow-going place to put you through your business-college term, so I am sure you are the man I'm looking for. I believe in helping those who have 'gumption' enough to help themselves, so we'll call it a bargain, Ned."

Their Girl Josie

HEN Paul Morgan, a rising young lawyer with justifiable political aspirations, married Elinor Ashton, leading woman at the Green Square Theatre, his old schoolmates and neighbours back in Spring Valley held up their hands in horror, and his father and mother up in the weather-grey Morgan homestead were crushed in the depths of humiliation. They had been too proud of Paul . . . their only son and such a clever fellow . . . and this was their punishment! He had married an actress! To Cyrus and Deborah Morgan, brought up and nourished all their lives on the strictest and straightest of old-fashioned beliefs both as regards this world and that which is to come, this was a tragedy.

They could not be brought to see it in any other light. As their neighbours said, "Cy Morgan never hilt up his head again after Paul married the play-acting woman." But perhaps it was less his humiliation than his sorrow which bowed down his erect form and sprinkled grey in his thick black hair that fifty years had hitherto spared. For Paul, forgetting the sacrifices his mother and father had made for him, had bitterly resented the letter of protest his father had written concerning his marriage. He wrote one angry, unfilial letter back and then came silence. Between grief and shame Cyrus and Deborah Morgan grew old rapidly in the year that followed.

At the end of that time Elinor Morgan, the mother of an hour, died; three months later Paul Morgan was killed in a railroad collision. After the funeral Cyrus Morgan brought home to his wife their son's little daughter, Joscelyn Morgan.

Her aunt, Annice Ashton, had wanted the baby. Cyrus Morgan had been almost rude in his refusal. His son's daughter should never be brought up by an actress; it was bad enough that her mother had been one and had doubtless transmitted the taint to her child. But in Spring Valley, if anywhere, it might be eradicated.

At first neither Cyrus nor Deborah cared much for Joscelyn. They resented her parentage, her strange, un-Morgan-like name, and the pronounced resemblance she bore to the dark-haired, dark-eyed mother they had never seen. All the Morgans had been fair. If Joscelyn had had Paul's blue eyes and golden curls her grandfather and grandmother would have loved her sooner.

But the love came . . . it had to. No living mortal could have resisted Joscelyn. She was the most winsome and lovable little mite of babyhood that ever toddled. Her big dark eyes overflowed with laughter before she could speak, her puckered red mouth broke constantly into dimples and cooing sounds. She had ways that no orthodox Spring Valley baby ever thought of having. Every smile was a caress, every gurgle of attempted speech a song. Her grandparents came to worship her and were stricter than ever with her by reason of their love. Because she was so dear to them she must be saved from her mother's blood.

Joscelyn shot up through a roly-poly childhood into slim, bewitching girlhood in a chill repressive atmosphere. Cyrus and Deborah were nothing if not thorough. The name of Joscelyn's mother was never mentioned to her; she was never called anything but Josie, which sounded more "Christian-like" than Joscelyn; and all the flowering out of her alien beauty was repressed as far as might be in the plainest and dullest of dresses and the primmest arrangement possible to riotous ripe-brown curls.

The girl was never allowed to visit her Aunt Annice, although frequently invited. Miss Ashton, however, wrote to her occasionally, and every Christmas sent a box of presents which even Cyrus and Deborah Morgan could not forbid her to accept, although they looked with disapproving eyes and ominously set lips at the dainty, frivolous trifles the actress woman sent. They would have liked to cast those painted fans and lace frills and beflounced lingerie into the fire as if they had been infected rags from a pest-house.

The path thus set for Joscelyn's dancing feet to walk in was indeed sedate and narrow. She was seldom allowed to mingle with the young people of even quiet, harmless Spring Valley; she was never allowed to attend local concerts, much less take part in them; she was forbidden to read novels, and Cyrus Morgan burned an old copy of Shakespeare which Paul had given him years ago and which he had himself read and treasured, lest its perusal should awaken unlawful instincts in Joscelyn's heart. The girl's passion for reading was so marked that her grandparents felt that it was their duty to repress it as far as lay in their power.

But Joscelyn's vitality was such that all her bonds and bands served but little to check or retard the growth of her rich nature. Do what they might they could not make a Morgan of her. Her every step was a dance, her every word and gesture full of a grace and virility that filled the old folks with uneasy wonder. She seemed to them charged with dangerous tendencies all the more potent from repression. She was sweet-tempered and sunny, truthful and modest, but she was as little like the trim, simple Spring Valley girls as a crimson rose is like a field daisy, and her unlikeness bore heavily on her grandparents.

Yet they loved her and were proud of her. "Our girl Josie," as they called her, was more to them than they would have admitted even to themselves, and in the main they were satisfied with her, although the grandmother grumbled because Josie did not take kindly to patchwork and rug-making and the grandfather would fain have toned down that exuberance of beauty and vivacity into the meeker pattern of maidenhood he had been accustomed to.

When Joscelyn was seventeen Deborah Morgan noticed a change in her. The girl became quieter and more brooding, falling at times into strange, idle reveries, with her hands clasped over her knee and her big eyes fixed unseeingly on space; or she would creep away for solitary rambles in the beech wood, going away droopingly and returning with dusky glowing cheeks and a nameless radiance, as of some newly discovered power, shining through every muscle and motion. Mrs. Morgan thought the child needed a tonic and gave her sulphur and molasses.

One day the revelation came. Cyrus and Deborah had driven across the valley to visit their married daughter. Not finding her at home they returned. Mrs. Morgan went into the house while her husband went to the stable. Joscelyn was not in the kitchen, but the grandmother heard the sound of voices and laughter in the sitting room across the hall.

"What company has Josie got?" she wondered, as she opened the hall door and paused for a moment on the threshold to listen. As she listened her old face grew grey and pinched; she turned noiselessly and left the house, and flew to her husband as one distracted.

"Cyrus, Josie is play-acting in the room . . . laughing and reciting and going on. I heard her. Oh, I've always feared it would break out in her and it has! Come you and listen to her."

The old couple crept through the kitchen and across the hall to the open parlour door as if they were stalking a thief. Joscelyn's laugh rang out as they did so . . . a mocking, triumphant peal. Cyrus and Deborah shivered as if they had heard sacrilege.

Joscelyn had put on a trailing, clinging black skirt which her aunt had sent her a year ago and which she had never been permitted to wear. It transformed her into a woman. She had cast aside her waist of dark plum-coloured homespun and wrapped a silken shawl about herself until only her beautiful arms and shoulders were left bare. Her hair, glossy and brown, with burnished red lights where the rays of the dull autumn sun struck on it through the window, was heaped high on her head and held in place by a fillet of pearl beads. Her cheeks were crimson, her whole body from head to foot instinct and alive with a beauty that to Cyrus and Deborah, as they stood mute with horror in the open doorway, seemed akin to some devilish enchantment.

Joscelyn, rapt away from her surroundings, did not perceive her grandparents. Her face was turned from them and she was addressing an unseen auditor in passionate denunciation. She spoke, moved, posed, gesticulated, with an inborn genius shining through every motion and tone like an illuminating lamp.

"Josie, what are you doing?"

It was Cyrus who spoke, advancing into the room like a stern, hard impersonation of judgment. Joscelyn's outstretched arm fell to her side and she turned sharply around; fear came into her face and the light went out of it. A moment before she had been a woman, splendid, unafraid; now she was again the schoolgirl, too confused and shamed to speak.

"What are you doing, Josie?" asked her grandfather again, "dressed up in that indecent manner and talking and twisting to yourself?"

Joscelyn's face, that had grown pale, flamed scarlet again. She lifted her head proudly.

"I was trying Aunt Annice's part in her new play," she answered. "I have not been doing anything wrong, Grandfather."

"Wrong! It's your mother's blood coming out in you, girl, in spite of all our care! Where did you get that play?"

"Aunt Annice sent it to me," answered Joscelyn, casting a quick glance at the book on the table. Then, when her grandfather picked it up gingerly, as if he feared contamination, she added quickly, "Oh, give it to me, please, Grandfather. Don't take it away."

"I am going to burn it," said Cyrus Morgan sternly.

"Oh, don't, Grandfather," cried Joscelyn, with a sob in her voice. "Don't burn it, please. I . . . I . . . won't practise out of it any more. I'm sorry I've displeased you. Please give me my book."

"No," was the stern reply. "Go to your room, girl, and take off that rig. There is to be no more play-acting in my house, remember that."

He flung the book into the fire that was burning in the grate. For the first time in her life Joscelyn flamed out into passionate defiance.

"You are cruel and unjust, Grandfather. I have done no wrong . . . it is not doing wrong to develop the one gift I have. It's the only thing I can do . . . and I am going to do it. My mother was an actress and a good woman. So is Aunt Annice. So I mean to be."

"Oh, Josie, Josie," said her grandmother in a scared voice. Her grandfather only repeated sternly, "Go, take that rig off, girl, and let us hear no more of this."

Joscelyn went but she left consternation behind her. Cyrus and Deborah could not have been more shocked if they had discovered the girl robbing her grandfather's desk. They talked the matter over bitterly at the kitchen hearth that night.

"We haven't been strict enough with the girl, Mother," said Cyrus angrily. "We'll have to be stricter if we don't want to have her disgracing us. Did you hear how she defied me? 'So I mean to be,' she says. Mother, we'll have trouble with that girl yet."

"Don't be too harsh with her, Pa . . . it'll maybe only drive her to worse," sobbed Deborah.

"I ain't going to be harsh. What I do is for her own good, you know that, Mother. Josie is as dear to me as she is to you, but we've got to be stricter with her."

They were. From that day Josie was watched and distrusted. She was never permitted to be alone. There were no more solitary walks. She felt herself under the surveillance of cold, unsympathetic eyes every moment and her very soul writhed. Joscelyn Morgan, the high-spirited daughter of high-spirited parents, could not long submit to such treatment. It might have passed with a child; to a woman, thrilling with life and conscious power to her very fingertips, it was galling beyond measure. Joscelyn rebelled, but she did nothing secretly . . . that was not her nature. She wrote to her Aunt Annice, and when she received her reply she went straight and fearlessly to her grandparents with it.

"Grandfather, this letter is from my aunt. She wishes me to go and live with her and prepare for the stage. I told her I wished to do so. I am going."

Cyrus and Deborah looked at her in mute dismay.

"I know you despise the profession of an actress," the girl went on with heightened colour. "I am sorry you think so about it because it is the only one open to me. I must go . . . I must."

"Yes, you must," said Cyrus cruelly. "It's in your blood . . . your bad blood, girl."

"My blood isn't bad," cried Joscelyn proudly. "My mother was a sweet, true, good woman. You are unjust, Grandfather. But I don't want you to be angry with me. I love you both and I am very grateful indeed for all your kindness to me. I wish that you could understand what . . ."

"We understand enough," interrupted Cyrus harshly. "This is all I have to say. Go to your play-acting aunt if you want to. Your grandmother and me won't hinder you. But you'll come back here no more. We'll have nothing further to do with you. You can choose your own way and walk in it."

With this dictum Joscelyn went from Spring Valley. She clung to Deborah and wept at parting, but Cyrus did not even say goodbye to her. On the morning of her departure he went away on business and did not return until evening.

JOSCELYN WENT ON THE STAGE. Her aunt's influence and her mother's fame helped her much. She missed the hard experiences that come to the unassisted beginner. But her own genius must have won in any case. She had all her mother's gifts, deepened by her inheritance of Morgan intensity and sincerity . . . much, too, of the Morgan firmness of will. When Joscelyn Morgan was twenty-two she was famous over two continents.

When Cyrus Morgan returned home on the evening after his granddaughter's departure he told his wife that she was never to mention the girl's name in his hearing again. Deborah obeyed. She thought her husband was right, albeit she might in her own heart deplore the necessity of such a decree. Joscelyn had disgraced them; could that be forgiven?

Nevertheless both the old people missed her terribly. The house seemed to have lost its soul with that vivid, ripely tinted young life. They got their married daughter's oldest girl, Pauline, to come and stay with them. Pauline was a quiet, docile maiden, industrious and commonplace – just such a girl as they had vainly striven to make of Joscelyn, to whom Pauline had always been held up as a model. Yet neither Cyrus nor Deborah took to her, and they let her go unregretfully when they found that she wished to return home.

"She hasn't any of Josie's gimp," was old Cyrus's unspoken fault. Deborah spoke, but all she said was, "Polly's a good girl, Father, only she hasn't any snap."

Joscelyn wrote to Deborah occasionally, telling her freely of her plans and doings. If it hurt the girl that no notice was ever taken of her letters she still wrote them. Deborah read the letters grimly and then left them in Cyrus's way. Cyrus would not read them at first; later on he read them stealthily when Deborah was out of the house.

When Joscelyn began to succeed she sent to the old farmhouse papers and magazines containing her photographs and criticisms of her plays and acting. Deborah cut them out and kept them in her upper bureau drawer with Joscelyn's letters. Once she overlooked one and Cyrus found it when he was kindling the fire. He got the scissors and cut it out carefully. A month later Deborah discovered it between the leaves of the family Bible.

But Joscelyn's name was never mentioned between them, and when other people asked them concerning her their replies were cold and ungracious. In a way they had relented towards her, but their shame of her remained. They could never forget that she was an actress.

Once, six years after Joscelyn had left Spring Valley, Cyrus, who was reading a paper by the table, got up with an angry exclamation and stuffed it into the stove, thumping the lid on over it with grim malignity.

"That fool dunno what he's talking about," was all he would say. Deborah had her share of curiosity. The paper was the *National Gazette* and she knew that their next-door neighbour, James Pennan, took it. She went over that evening and borrowed it, saying that their own had been burned before she had had time to read the serial in it. With one exception she read all its columns carefully without finding anything to explain her husband's anger. Then she doubtfully plunged into the exception . . . a column of "Stage Notes." Halfway down she came upon an adverse criticism of Joscelyn Morgan and her new play. It was malicious and vituperative. Deborah Morgan's old eyes sparkled dangerously as she read it.

"I guess somebody is pretty jealous of Josie," she muttered. "I don't wonder Pa was riled up. But I guess she can hold her own. She's a Morgan."

No long time after this Cyrus took a notion he'd like a trip to the city. He'd like to see the Horse Fair and look up Cousin Hiram Morgan's folks.

"Hiram and me used to be great chums, Mother. And we're getting kind of mossy, I guess, never stirring out of Spring Valley. Let's go and dissipate for a week – what say?"

Deborah agreed readily, albeit of late years she had been much averse to going far from home and had never at any time been very fond of Cousin Hiram's wife. Cyrus was as pleased as a child over their trip. On the second day of their sojourn in the city he slipped away when Deborah had gone shopping with Mrs. Hiram and hurried through the streets to the Green Square Theatre with a hang-dog look. He bought a ticket apologetically and sneaked in to his seat. It was a matinee performance, and Joscelyn Morgan was starring in her famous new play.

Cyrus waited for the curtain to rise, feeling as if every one of his Spring Valley neighbours must know where he was and revile him for it. If Deborah were ever to find out . . . but Deborah must never find out! For the first time in their married life the old man deliberately plotted to deceive his old wife. He must see his girl Josie just once; it was a terrible thing that she was an actress, but she was a successful one, nobody could deny that, except fools who yapped in the *National Gazette.*

The curtain went up and Cyrus rubbed his eyes. He had certainly braced his nerves to behold some mystery of iniquity; instead he saw an old kitchen so like his own at home that it bewildered him; and there, sitting by the cheery wood stove, in homespun gown, with primly braided hair, was Joscelyn – his girl Josie, as he had seen her a thousand times by his own ingle-side. The building rang with applause; one old man pulled out a red bandanna and wiped tears of joy and pride from his eyes. She hadn't changed – Josie hadn't changed. Play-acting hadn't spoiled her – couldn't spoil her. Wasn't she Paul's daughter! And all this applause was for her – for Josie.

Joscelyn's new play was a homely, pleasant production

with rollicking comedy and heart-moving pathos skilfully commingled. Joscelyn pervaded it all with a convincing simplicity that was really the triumph of art. Cyrus Morgan listened and exulted in her; at every burst of applause his eyes gleamed with pride. He wanted to go on the stage and box the ears of the villain who plotted against her; he wanted to shake hands with the good woman who stood by her; he wanted to pay off the mortgage and make Josie happy. He wiped tears from his eyes in the third act when Josie was turned out of doors and, when the fourth left her a happy, blushing bride, hand in hand with her farmer lover, he could have wept again for joy.

Cyrus Morgan went out into the daylight feeling as if he had awakened from a dream. At the outer door he came upon Mrs. Hiram and Deborah. Deborah's face was stained with tears, and she caught at his hand.

"Oh, Pa, wasn't it splendid – wasn't our girl Josie splendid! I'm so proud of her. Oh, I was bound to hear her. I was afraid you'd be mad, so I didn't let on and when I saw you in the seat down there I couldn't believe my eyes. Oh, I've just been crying the whole time. Wasn't it splendid! Wasn't our girl Josie splendid?"

The crowd around looked at the old pair with amused, indulgent curiosity, but they were quite oblivious to their surroundings, even to Mrs. Hiram's anxiety to decoy them away. Cyrus Morgan cleared his throat and said, "It was great, Mother, great. She took the shine off the other play-actors all right. I knew that *National Gazette* man didn't know what he was talking about. Mother, let us go and see Josie right off. She's stopping with her aunt at the Maberly Hotel – I saw it in the paper this morning. I'm going to tell her she was right and we were wrong. Josie's beat them all, and I'm going to tell her so!"

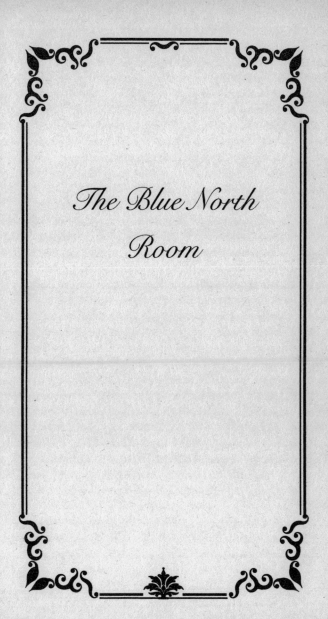

The Blue North

Room

HIS," said Sara, laying Aunt Josephina's letter down on the kitchen table with such energy that in anybody but Sara it must have been said she threw it down, "this is positively the last straw! I have endured all the rest. I have given up my chance of a musical education, when Aunt Nan offered it, that I might stay home and help Willard pay the mortgage off – if it doesn't pay us off first – and I have, which was much harder, accepted the fact that we can't possibly afford to send Ray to the Valley Academy, even if I wore the same hat and coat for four winters. I did not grumble when Uncle Joel came here to live because he wanted to be 'near his dear nephew's children.' I felt it my Christian duty to look pleasant when we had to give Cousin Caroline a home to save her from the poorhouse. But my endurance and philosophy, and worst of all, my furniture, has reached a limit. I cannot have Aunt Josephina come here to spend the winter, because I have no room to put her in."

"Hello, Sally, what's the matter?" asked Ray, coming in with a book. It would have been hard to catch Ray without a book; he generally took one even to bed with him. Ray had a headful of brains, and Sara thought it was a burning shame that there seemed to be no chance for his going to college. "You look all rumpled up in your conscience, beloved sis," the boy went on, chaffingly.

"My conscience is all right," said Sara severely. "It's worse than that. If you please, here's a letter from Aunt Josephina! She writes that she is very lonesome. Her son has gone to South America, and won't be back until spring, and she wants to come and spend the winter with us."

"Well, why not?" asked Ray serenely. Nothing ever bothered Ray. "The more the merrier."

"Ray Sheldon! Where are we to put her? We have no spare room, as you well know."

"Can't she room with Cousin Caroline?"

"Cousin Caroline's room is too small for two. It's full to overflowing with her belongings now, and Aunt Josephina will bring two trunks at least. Try again, bright boy."

"What's the matter with the blue north room?"

"There is nothing the matter with it – oh, nothing at all! We could put Aunt Josephina there, but where will she sleep? Where will she wash her face? Will it not seem slightly inhospitable to invite her to sit on a bare floor? Have you forgotten that there isn't a stick of furniture in the blue north room and, worse still, that we haven't a spare cent to buy any, not even the cheapest kind?"

"I'll give it up," said Ray. "I might have a try at squaring the circle if you asked me, but the solution of the Aunt Josephina problem is beyond me."

"The solution is simply that we must write to Aunt Josephina, politely but firmly, that we can't have her come, owing to lack of accommodation. You must write the letter, Ray. Make it as polite as you can, but above all make it firm."

"Oh, but Sally, dear," protested Ray, who didn't relish having to write such a letter, "isn't this rather hasty, rather inhospitable? Poor Aunt Josephina must really be rather lonely, and it's only natural she should want to visit her relations."

"We're *not* her relations," cried Sara. "We're not a speck of relation really. She's only the half-sister of Mother's half-brother. That sounds nice and relationy, doesn't it? And she's fussy and interfering, and she will fight with Cousin Caroline, everybody fights with Cousin Caroline –"

"Except Sara," interrupted Ray, but Sara went on with a rush, "And we won't have a minute's peace all winter. Anyhow, where could we put her even if we wanted her to come? No, we can't have her!"

"Mother was always very fond of Aunt Josephina," said Ray reflectively. Sara had her lips open, all ready to answer whatever Ray might say, but she shut them suddenly and the boy went on. "Aunt Josephina thought a lot of Mother, too.

She used to say she knew there was always a welcome for her at Maple Hollow. It does seem a pity, Sally dear, for your mother's daughter to send word to Aunt Josephina, per my mother's son, that there isn't room for her any longer at Maple Hollow."

"I shall leave it to Willard," said Sara abruptly. "If he says to let her come, come she shall, even if Dorothy and I have to camp in the barn."

"I'm going to have a prowl around the garret," said Ray, apropos of nothing.

"And I shall get the tea ready," answered Sara briskly. "Dorothy will be home from school very soon, and I hear Uncle Joel stirring. Willard won't be back till dark, so there is no use waiting for him."

At twilight Sara decided to walk up the lane and meet Willard. She always liked to meet him thus when he had been away for a whole day. Sara thought there was nobody in the world as good and dear as Willard.

It was a dull grey November twilight; the maples in the hollow were all leafless, and the hawthorn hedge along the lane was sere and frosted; a little snow had fallen in the afternoon, and lay in broad patches on the brown fields. The world looked very dull and dispirited, and Sara sighed. She could not help thinking of the dark side of things just then. "Everything is wrong," said poor Sara dolefully. "Willard has to work like a slave, and yet with all his efforts he can barely pay the interest on the mortgage. And Ray ought to go to college. But I don't see how we can ever manage. To be sure, he won't be ready until next fall, but we won't have the money then any more than now. It would take every bit of a hundred and fifty dollars to fit him out with books and clothes, and pay for board and tuition at the academy. If he could just have a year there he could teach and earn his own way through college. But we might as well hope for the moon as one hundred and fifty dollars."

Sara sighed again. She was only eighteen, but she felt very old. Willard was nineteen, and Willard had never had a chance to be young. His father had died when he was twelve, and he had run the farm since then, he and Sara together indeed, for Sara was a capital planner and manager and worker. The little mother had died two years ago, and the household cares had all fallen on Sara's shoulders since. Sometimes, as now, they pressed very heavily, but a talk with Willard always heartened her up. Willard had his blue spells too, but Sara thought it a special Providence that their blue turns never came together. When one got downhearted the other was always ready to do the cheering up.

Sara was glad to hear Willard whistling when he drove into the lane; it was a sign he was in good spirits. He pulled up, and Sara climbed into the wagon.

"Things go all right today, Sally?" he asked cheerfully.

"There was a letter from Aunt Josephina," answered Sara, anxious to get the worst over, "and she wants to come to Maple Hollow for the winter. I thought at first we just couldn't have her, but I decided to leave it to you."

"Well, we've got a pretty good houseful already," said Willard thoughtfully. "But I suppose if Aunt Josephina wants to come we'd better have her. I always liked Aunt Josephina, and so did Mother, you know."

"I don't know where we can put her. We haven't any spare room, Will."

"Ray and I can sleep in the kitchen loft. You and Dolly take our room, and let Aunt Josephina take yours."

"The kitchen loft isn't really fit to sleep in," said Sara pessimistically. "It's awfully cold, and there're mice and rats – ugh! You and Ray will get nibbled in spots. But it's the only thing to do if we must have Aunt Josephina. I'll get Ray to write to her tomorrow. I couldn't put enough cordiality into the letter if I wrote it myself."

Ray came in while Willard was at supper. There were

cobwebs all over him from his head to his heels. "I've solved the Aunt J. problem," he announced cheerfully. "We will furnish the blue north room."

"With what?" asked Sara disbelievingly.

"I've been poking about in the garret and in the carriage house loft," said Ray, "and I've found furniture galore. It's very old and cobwebby – witness my appearance – and very much in want of scrubbing and a few nails. But it will do."

"I'd forgotten about those old things," said Sara slowly. "They've never been used since I can remember, and long before. They were discarded before Mother came here. But I thought they were all broken and quite useless."

"Not at all. I believe we can furbish them up sufficiently to make the room habitable. It will be rather old-fashioned, but then it's Hobson's choice. There are the pieces of an old bed out in the loft, and they can be put together. There's an old corner cupboard out there too, with leaded glass doors, two old solid wooden armchairs, and a funny old chest of drawers with a writing desk in place of the top drawer, all full of yellow old letters and trash. I found it under a pile of old carpet. Then there's a washstand, and also a towel rack up in the garret, and the funniest old table with three claw legs, and a tippy top. One leg is broken off, but I hunted around and found it, and I guess we can fix it on. And there are two more old chairs and a queer little oval table with a cracked swing mirror on it."

"I have it," exclaimed Sara, with a burst of inspiration, "let us fix up a real old-fashioned room for Aunt Josephina. It won't do to put anything modern with those old things. One would kill the other. I'll put Mother's rag carpet down in it, and the four braided mats Grandma Sheldon gave me, and the old brass candlestick and the Irish chain coverlet. Oh, I believe it will be lots of fun."

It was. For a week the Sheldons hammered and glued and washed and consulted. The north room was already papered with a blue paper of an old-fashioned stripe-and-diamond pattern. The rag carpet was put down, and the braided rugs laid on it. The old bedstead was set up in one corner and, having been well cleaned and polished with beeswax and turpentine, was really a handsome piece of furniture. On the washstand Sara placed a quaint old basin and ewer which had been Grandma Sheldon's. Ray had fixed up the table as good as new; Sara had polished the brass claws, and on the table she put the brass tray, two candlesticks, and snuffers which had been long stowed away in the kitchen loft. The dressing table and swing mirror, with its scroll frame of tarnished gilt, was in the window corner, and opposite it was the old chest of drawers. The cupboard was set up in a corner, and beside it stood the spinning-wheel from the kitchen loft. The big grandfather clock, which had always stood in the hall below, was carried up, and two platters of blue willow-ware were set up over the mantel. Above them was hung the faded sampler that Grandma Sheldon had worked ninety years ago when she was a little girl.

"Do you know," said Sara, when they stood in the middle of the room and surveyed the result, "I expected to have a good laugh over this, but it doesn't look funny after all. The things all seem to suit each other, some way, and they look good, don't they? I mean they look *real*, clear through. I believe that table and those drawers are solid mahogany. And look at the carving on those bedposts. Cleaning them has made such a difference. I do hope Aunt Josephina won't mind their being so old."

Aunt Josephina didn't. She was very philosophical about it when Sara explained that Cousin Caroline had the spare room, and the blue north room was all they had left. "Oh, it will be all right," she said, plainly determined to make the best of things. "Those old things are thought a lot of now, anyhow. I can't say I fancy them much myself – I like something a little brighter. But the rich folks have gone cracked over them. I know a woman in Boston that's got her whole house furnished with old truck, and as soon as she hears of any old furniture anywhere she's not contented till she's got it. She says it's her hobby, and she spends a heap on it. She'd be in raptures if she saw this old room of yours, Sary."

"Do you mean," said Sara slowly, "that there are people who would buy old things like these?"

"Yes, and pay more for them than would buy a real nice set with a marble-topped burey. You may well say there's lots of fools in the world, Sary." Sara was not saying or thinking any such thing. It was a new idea to her that any value was attached to old furniture, for Sara lived very much out of the world of fads and collectors. But she did not forget what Aunt Josephina had said.

The winter passed away. Aunt Josephina plainly enjoyed her visit, whatever the Sheldons felt about it. In March her son returned, and Aunt Josephina went home to him. Before she left, Sara asked her for the address of the woman whose hobby was old furniture, and the very afternoon after Aunt Josephina had gone Sara wrote and mailed a letter. For a week she looked so mysterious that Willard and Ray could not guess what she was plotting. At the end of that time Mrs. Stanton came.

Mrs. Stanton always declared afterwards that the mere sight of that blue north room gave her raptures. Such a find! Such a discovery! A bedstead with carved posts, a claw-footed table, real old willow-ware plates with the birds' bills meeting! Here was luck, if you like!

When Willard and Ray came home to tea Sara was sitting on the stairs counting her wealth.

"Sally, where did you discover all that long-lost treasure?" demanded Ray.

"Mrs. Stanton of Boston was here today," said Sara, enjoying the moment of revelation hugely. "She makes a hobby of collecting old furniture. I sold her every blessed thing in the blue north room except Mother's carpet and Grandma's mats and sampler. She wanted those too, but I couldn't part with them. She bought everything else and," Sara lifted her hands, full of bills, dramatically, "here are two hundred and fifty dollars to take you to the Valley Academy next fall, Ray."

"It wouldn't be fair to take it for that," said Ray, flushing. "You and Will—"

"Will and I say you must take it," said Sara. "Don't we, Will? There is nothing we want so much as to give you a college start. It is an enormous burden off my mind to think it is so nicely provided for. Besides, most of those old things were yours by the right of rediscovery, and you voted first of all to have Aunt Josephina come."

"You must take it, of course, Ray," said Willard. "Nothing else would give Sara and me so much pleasure. A blessing on Aunt Josephina."

"Amen," said Sara and Ray.

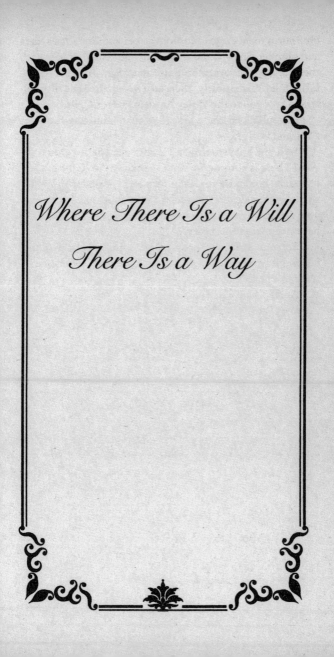

Where There Is a Will
There Is a Way

ORDON heard the key click in the lock. He sprang to the door.

"Aunt Mary – Aunt Mary!" he called.

There was no answer – nothing save the sound of his aunt's heavy boots clattering down the back stairs.

Gordon sat down on a broken-backed chair and looked grim. He knew, as he expressed it, what he was up against. Aunt Mary had evidently determined that he should not take part in the debate. And he had promised Mr. Leckie that he would be there without fail.

He felt no particular indignation against Aunt Mary. It was just what he might have expected, and he should have been on his guard. Anyway, he had no time or energy to waste in being angry. The first thing to do was to find a way to escape and keep his promise. Nevertheless, he felt that Aunt Mary had not treated him fairly. She had never forbidden him to take part in the debate, although she let it be seen plainly that she thought it all rank foolishness. And now, when he had run down the hall to the little box-room to look for a certain book, she had snatched the chance to lock him in. Aunt Mary did things like that.

Gordon went to the little square window and looked out into the bleak November night. The ancient creeper, with stems as thick as his arm, wandered over the side of the house. Nobody had ever tried to climb down it before, but there had to be a first time for everything. Gordon thought he might risk it. But the clothes problem was more serious. He had nothing on but his underclothes and his socks. Now it was manifestly out of the question to appear on the auditorium platform of the high school in such a costume, even if one could walk four miles on a cold night in it. To be sure, he might borrow something from the Ewarts. But the Ewarts were no friends of Aunt Mary's, and Gordon would not ask favours of them on that account.

Aunt Mary Holland was what was known locally as a "character." She was a gaunt woman of sixty-five, who ran her own little farm with Gordon's assistance, and seemed to be on bad terms with all her neighbours. She had "raised" Gordon's father and, after his death and his wife's death, she had "raised" Gordon. She was the only relative he had and, in spite of her queer ways and her grimness, he was rather fond of her. She did not seem to be at all fond of him, and he knew exactly what opinion she had of his father. She had sent him to the public school until he was fourteen, and these past three years she had let him go to the high school in Exeter. But she gave him to understand that would be all. No college nonsense for her.

"If you'd help me to get a start, Aunt Mary," said Gordon, "I'd be able to work my own way through."

"Your father was always going to do wonderful things," said Aunt Mary. "Only, somehow, he never did 'em. Mark Abbey will want a clerk in his dry-goods store next summer. I think that's about your measure. You'll go there when the year ends."

Gordon had not made many friends at the high school. Aunt Mary disapproved of all amusements and sports, and he would not anger her by going in for them. But his teachers liked the quiet, studious lad, and Mr. Leckie, the principal, had taken a special interest in him ever since he had found out that Gordon had the makings of a good debater. When the Croyden High School had challenged the Exeter school to a debate Gordon was chosen to open it. He had worked hard over his speech and his "points," and he knew Mr. Leckie depended on him to win the debate.

"I've got to be there," said Gordon.

The only clothes in the box-room were a dark green serge dress of very ancient vintage and an old shabby "duster" hanging on the wall. Gordon put on the dress. He was tall and Aunt Mary was short, so that the dress came no further than his knees. The duster covered it very well and, being longer, came well below the tops of his socks. Gordon found a pair of his own discarded boots in a box. They were worn and unpolished, but no better were to be had. Perhaps if he could get to Exeter in time he might call at Tom Purdee's, explain his predicament, and borrow something decent. Tom was the only high-school boy Gordon knew at all well.

"And now," said Gordon, "the best way to get there is to start."

The window went up stiffly. The creeper-stems were tough, and Gordon soon found himself on the ground. The kitchen light burned, so there was no use in thinking of trying to slip into the house and get some clothes. Besides, he had very little time. Only an hour – and it would take him all that to walk into Exeter. It was four miles by the road.

Then Gordon thought of the winter short-cut over the fields and across the river. It was used only when the river was frozen. But if he could cross on one of the stringers of the old dismantled bridge, he could save fifteen minutes, and fifteen minutes would allow him to call at Tom's. Nobody had ever crossed on the stringer that he knew of, but he thought it could be done. It would, of course, be more difficult at night, but there was a moon.

When he arrived at the river his grit almost failed him. Suppose he fell off! There was every chance that he would. But to go all the way back and around by the road meant that he would be half an hour late.

Gordon wrapped his draperies closely around him and crossed on the right-hand stringer. Fortunately the night was calm. Twice he almost slipped off. There was a dew of perspiration on his face when he reached the other side.

"I don't believe I'd want to do that again," he said, as he sprang ashore.

He had saved half an hour. With luck he could get to Exeter in time to hunt up Tom Purdee and borrow a pair of trousers.

As he emerged from the woods beyond the river and climbed the fence to the highway he saw something black and furry stretched by the roadside. It was a dog that whined as Gordon bent over it. The poor beast had something wrong with its leg – probably broken by some passing car.

Gordon sighed. But it never occurred to him that he could leave the poor creature there to suffer. He picked it up carefully in his arms and started on again. He knew he could not get to Tom's now. He must take the dog to old Doctor Vernon, the veterinary, who lived at the other end of the town. When this was done and the kindly old man had promised to do his best for the dog, it was ten minutes past eight by the town clock and the debate was to have begun at eight. It took Gordon ten more minutes to reach the school. He found the rather excitable Mr. Leckie half frantic.

"What on earth kept you, Gordon? Everybody is waiting."

"I was unfortunately delayed," said Gordon calmly.

"Well, you are here at last, thank goodness. Hurry up and get your coat off and get in."

"I think I'll keep my coat on," said Gordon, moving along.

Mr. Leckie stared. Then shrugged his shoulders and started after Gordon resignedly. The fellow was as queer as his old great-aunt. But he had brains and he could debate and Mr. Leckie expected him to wipe up the floor with the Croyden team. Not that Mr. Leckie, even in thought, used such an expression, but that was the gist of it.

Gordon knew what sort of a figure he cut on the platform in that shabby old duster and those terrible shoes. He knew his fellow debaters were ashamed of him, and he saw the derision and contempt in the eyes of the Croyden boys. They considered the debate as good as won.

Well, he would show them.

Nevertheless, when he stood up, he had a few moments of panic. He could think of nothing but the old green dress under the duster. It seemed as if everybody could see it. Mr. Leckie fairly groaned with impatience. Suppose the fellow flunked at this last moment! That shabby old duster! Hadn't the boy a decent overcoat? But the face above the frayed collar was flushed and handsome and strong-jawed, with a mane of black hair over it. If he would only open his mouth!

Just then Gordon saw Aunt Mary at the back of the auditorium. What ever had brought her there? She despised such goings-on. Yet there she sat, in a ridiculous old bonnet and an equally ridiculous old velvet mantle. And yet, although Aunt Mary always wore ridiculous things, she never looked ridiculous. Her face was too strong and vigorous for that.

Well, he was not going to fail before Aunt Mary. Gordon got his mouth open at last.

They talk of that debate yet. At least, Exeter people do. The Croyden folks don't. They hadn't the ghost of a chance when Gordon got going. He forgot his serge dress and the duster and the hole in the toe of his boot. And everybody else forgot them – or what they could see of them. Such a speech had never been made in Exeter High before.

"I knew you could do something, but I didn't know you could do *that*," said Mr. Leckie, as he wrung Gordon's hand at the close.

Aunt Mary pushed up through the crowd. "I've got the horse and the buckboard here," she said curtly, "if you want to drive home."

They drove home in absolute silence. Gordon wondered if Aunt Mary were very angry. One could never tell. When he had put away the horse and gone in he found her standing in the kitchen.

"Well, you kept your promise," said Aunt Mary. "I didn't think you had it in you. Your father never kept a promise – *that* I know to my cost. And he sat down and wept over every little difficulty. As for pride – he'd never have gone to Exeter in my old serge dress and that duster. When I found you'd got out – I was out by the duck-house when you came sprawling down the vines – I hitched up and started for Exeter. I thought maybe you'd something worth saying since you were so set on saying it. How come I didn't overtake you on the road?"

"I went by the old river road."

"The old river road? But the ice hasn't made yet."

"I crossed on a stringer of the old bridge."

Aunt Mary stared at him. "My stars, think of that! You crossed on a stringer! Why, weren't you scared?"

"Of course," said Gordon.

Aunt Mary smiled in her usual grim fashion. "If you'd said you weren't frightened I'd have known you for a liar. But to be scared *and* cross it! Well, you'd be wasted behind a counter. I'll sell that piece of pine wood. It'll give you a start – and I ain't afraid any longer that you wouldn't keep on. No, the only trouble'd be to stop you."

Lilian's Business

Venture

ILIAN MITCHELL turned into the dry-goods store on Randall Street, just as Esther Miller and Ella Taylor came out. They responded coldly to her greeting and exchanged significant glances as they walked away.

Lilian's pale face crimsoned. She was a tall, slender girl of about seventeen, and dressed in mourning. These girls had been her close friends once. But that was before the Mitchells had lost their money. Since then Lilian had been cut by many of her old chums and she felt it keenly.

The clerks in the store were busy and Lilian sat down to wait her turn. Near to her two ladies were also waiting and chatting.

"Helen wants me to let her have a birthday party," Mrs. Saunders was saying wearily. "She has been promised it so long and I hate to disappoint the child, but our girl left last week, and I cannot possibly make all the cakes and things myself. I haven't the time or strength, so Helen must do without her party."

"Talking of girls," said Mrs. Reeves impatiently, "I am almost discouraged. It is so hard to get a good all-round one. The last one I had was so saucy I had to discharge her, and the one I have now cannot make decent bread. I never had good luck with bread myself either."

"That is Mrs. Porter's great grievance too. It is no light task to bake bread for all those boarders. Have you made your jelly yet?"

"No. Maria cannot make it, she says, and I detest messing with jelly. But I really must see to it soon."

At this point a saleswoman came up to Lilian, who made her small purchases and went out.

"There goes Lilian Mitchell," said Mrs. Reeves in an undertone. "She looks very pale. They say they are dreadfully poor since Henry Mitchell died. His affairs were in a bad condition, I am told."

"I am sorry for Mrs. Mitchell," responded Mrs. Saunders. "She is such a sweet woman. Lilian will have to do something, I suppose, and there is so little chance for a girl here."

Lilian, walking down the street, was wearily turning over in her mind the problems of her young existence. Her father had died the preceding spring. He had been a supposedly prosperous merchant; the Mitchells had always lived well, and Lilian was a petted and only child. Then came the shock of Henry Mitchell's sudden death and of financial ruin. His affairs were found to be hopelessly involved; when all the debts were paid there was left only the merest pittance – barely enough for house-rent – for Lilian and her mother to live upon. They had moved into a tiny cottage in an unfashionable locality, and during the summer Lilian had tried hard to think of something to do. Mrs. Mitchell was a delicate woman, and the burden of their situation fell on Lilian's young shoulders.

There seemed to be no place for her. She could not teach and had no particular talent in any line. There was no opening for her in Willington, which was a rather sleepy little place, and Lilian was almost in despair.

"There really doesn't seem to be any real place in the world for me, Mother," she said rather dolefully at the supper table. "I've no talent at all; it is dreadful to have been born without one. And yet I *must* do something, and do it soon."

And Lilian, after she had washed up the tea dishes, went upstairs and had a good cry.

But the darkest hour, so the proverb goes, is just before the dawn, and after Lilian had had her cry out and was sitting at her window in the dusk, watching a thin new moon shining over the trees down the street, her inspiration came to her. A minute later she whirled into the tiny sitting-room where her mother was sewing.

"Mother, our fortune is made! I have an idea!"

"Don't lose it, then," said Mrs. Mitchell with a smile. "What is it, my dear?"

Lilian sobered herself, sat down by her mother's side, and proceeded to recount the conversation she had heard in the store that afternoon.

"Now, Mother, this is where my brilliant idea comes in. You have often told me I am a born cook and I always have good luck. Now, tomorrow morning I shall go to Mrs. Saunders and offer to furnish all the good things for Helen's birthday party, and then I'll ask Mrs. Reeves and Mrs. Porter if I may make their bread for them. That will do for a beginning. I like cooking, you know, and I believe that in time I can work up a good business."

"It seems to be a good idea," said Mrs. Mitchell thoughtfully, "and I am willing that you should try. But have you thought it all out carefully? There will be many difficulties."

"I know. I don't expect smooth sailing right along, and perhaps I'll fail altogether; but somehow I don't believe I will."

"A great many of your old friends will think –"

"Oh, yes; I know *that* too, but I am not going to mind it, Mother. I don't think there is any disgrace in working for my living. I'm going to do my best and not care what people say."

Early next morning Lilian started out. She had carefully thought over the details of her small venture, considered ways and means, and decided on the most advisable course. She would not attempt too much, and she felt sure of success.

To secure competent servants was one of the problems of Willington people. At Drayton, a large neighbouring town, were several factories, and into these all the working girls from Willington had crowded, leaving very few who were willing to go out to service. Many of those who did were poor cooks, and Lilian shrewdly suspected that many a harassed housekeeper in the village would be glad to avail herself of the new enterprise.

Lilian was, as she had said of herself, "a born cook." This was her capital, and she meant to make the most of it. Mrs. Saunders listened to her businesslike details with surprise and delight.

"It is the very thing," she said. "Helen is so eager for that party, but I could not undertake it myself. Her birthday is Friday. Can you have everything ready by then?"

"Yes, I think so," said Lilian briskly, producing her notebook. "Please give me the list of what you want and I will do my best."

From Mrs. Saunders she went to Mrs. Reeves and found a customer as soon as she had told the reason of her call. "I'll furnish all the bread and rolls you need," she said, "and they will be good, too. Now, about your jelly. I can make good jelly, and I'll be very glad to make yours."

When she left, Lilian had an order for two dozen glasses of apple jelly, as well as a standing one for bread and rolls. Mrs. Porter was next visited and grasped eagerly at the opportunity.

"I know your bread will be good," she said, "and you may count on me as a regular customer."

Lilian thought she had enough on hand for a first attempt and went home satisfied. On her way she called at the grocery store with an order that surprised Mr. Hooper. When she told him of her plan he opened his eyes.

"I must tell my wife about that. She isn't strong and she doesn't like cooking."

After dinner Lilian went to work, enveloped in a big apron, and whipped eggs, stoned raisins, stirred, concocted, and baked until dark. When bedtime came she was so tired that she could hardly crawl upstairs; but she felt happy too, for the day had been a successful one.

And so also were the days and weeks and months that followed. It was hard and constant work, but it brought its reward. Lilian had not promised more than she could perform, and her customers were satisfied. In a short time she found herself with a regular and growing business on her hands, for new customers were gradually added and always came to stay.

People who gave parties found it very convenient to follow Mrs. Saunders's example and order their supplies from Lilian. She had a very busy winter and, of course, it was not all plain sailing. She had many difficulties to contend with. Sometimes days came on which everything seemed to go wrong – when the stove smoked or the oven wouldn't heat properly, when cakes fell flat and bread was sour and pies behaved as only totally depraved pies can, when she burned her fingers and felt like giving up in despair.

Then, again, she found herself cut by several of her old acquaintances. But she was too sensible to worry much over this. The friends really worth having were still hers, her mother's face had lost its look of care, and her business was prospering. She was hopeful and wide awake, kept her wits about her and looked out for hints, and learned to laugh over her failures.

During the winter she and her mother had managed to do most of the work themselves, hiring little Mary Robinson next door on especially busy days, and now and then calling in the assistance of Jimmy Bowen and his hand sled to carry orders to customers. But when spring came Lilian prepared to open up her summer campaign on a much larger scale. Mary Robinson was hired for the season, and John Perkins was engaged to act as carrier with his express wagon. A summer kitchen was boarded in in the backyard, and a new range bought; Lilian began operations with a striking advertisement in the Willington *News* and an attractive circular sent around to all her patrons. Picnics and summer weddings were frequent. In bread and rolls her trade was brisk and constant.

She also took orders for pickles, preserves, and jellies, and this became such a flourishing branch that a second assistant had to be hired.

It was a cardinal rule with Lilian never to send out any article that was not up to her standard. She bore the loss of her failures, and sometimes stayed up half of the night to fill an order on time. "Prompt and perfect" was her motto.

The long hot summer days were very trying, and sometimes she got very tired of it all. But when on the anniversary of her first venture she made up her accounts she was well pleased. To be sure, she had not made a fortune; but she had paid all their expenses, had a hundred dollars clear, and had laid the solid foundations of a profitable business.

"Mother," she said jubilantly, as she wiped a dab of flour from her nose and proceeded to concoct the icing for Blanche Remington's wedding cake, "don't you think my business venture has been a decided success?"

Mrs. Mitchell surveyed her busy daughter with a motherly smile. "Yes, I think it has," she said.

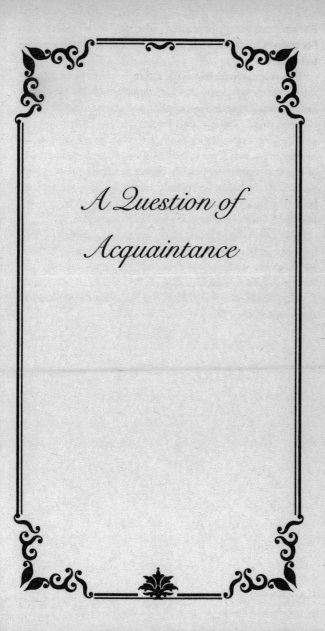

A Question of

Acquaintance

HE FIDDLE was at the bottom of it all. If Dr. James Dimma had not been awakened in the "wee sma's" by the sound of a violin on the porch of Miss Jackson's bungalow next door he might have forgiven Arthur Binns for other things. For looking like a movie star; for asking him ten days before, "Caught anything yet?" when Dr. Dimma had been on the lake for three mortal hours without a bite; for – most unforgivable thing of all – being evidently poor and certainly unknown.

But to be wakened out of a sound and much needed sleep at three o'clock a.m. by such ungodly caterwauling was too much. Yes, by gad, far too much. Something had to be done about it. Where the devil had Miss Jackson gone, and why had she left this jackanapes in her house while she was away? Had she left him? He had come there the day after she had gone. Perhaps she didn't know a thing about it. He might be a bank bandit. Likely he was. Nobody but a bank bandit would play a fiddle on the porch at three o'clock in the morning. And Merle was getting too friendly with him – far too friendly. Hadn't he seen her throwing a rose at the fellow over the hedge the night before? To be sure, Merle threw roses at everybody. But to throw them to an unknown nobody who probably hadn't a doctor in his family for generations back! No, this must be put a stop to at once. Merle could have her own way about the boys she played round with up to a certain point, but there was a limit. No more roses – no more going off to play golf together at the Sangamo Club. There had been two weeks of this, but it was going to stop. Dr. Dimma hadn't the least doubt that it would stop when he said so. Merle was the most docile, the most pliable of girls. She had always done what he told her to do. She would, he hadn't the least doubt, eventually marry Clark Fairweather when he told her to. No girl in her senses would dream of refusing Clark. Oodles of money; a pedigree equal to the Dimmas' for antiquity; a hard-working fellow with a professional chair waiting for him. To be sure, he wasn't a doctor. Dr. Dimma sighed as he pulled off his purple-and-orange pyjamas, rolled them into a savage ball, and hurled them on the floor. That would be too much good luck for such a contrary world.

Dr. Dimma worshipped his own profession. No other counted for much in his eyes. He had always hoped Merle would marry a doctor. To have a son-in-law with whom he could discuss germs and operations and cancers would have been the height of bliss in his eyes. And there had been no lack of candidates. Merle could even have had Cleaver Robinson, whose researches into various elusive bacilli had already put him in the limelight. To be sure, poor Cleaver looked rather like a magnified bacillus himself. No wonder Merle couldn't bear him. Dr. Dimma was not an unreasonable parent. But there was no fault to be found with Clark Fairweather personally, and it was high time Merle stopped her shilly-shallying with all the boys in Sangamo and settled down.

And no more roses over the fence. He'd see to that at once. Was he growing roses to see them wasted that way on a fellow who couldn't tell a Gloire de Dijon from a cabbage rose? Weren't they enough trouble and worriment without that? He didn't see why he wasted time and energy over the beastly things. Slugs – and spiders – and blight – and mildew! Any man was a fool who made a hobby of rose-growing. Any man was a fool to give his daughter so much of her own way. He'd show her!

And Dr. Dimma, who worshipped Merle and would have died if he couldn't grow roses, went down to breakfast in an atrocious humour with everything and everybody, and determined to make them feel it.

To make thing worse, Merle was ten minutes late and told him his watch was wrong. It infuriated Dr. Dimma ever to be told his watch was wrong. He pounded the table and glared at her. Not that Merle cared. She was not in the least afraid of her father, though she had spent the most of her young life luring him to make up his mind as she wanted it made up, and explaining away his insulting remarks to her friends. Even now, behind his glare his pride in her was fairly sticking out of his bulging blue eyes. Not another girl in Sangamo was a patch on her. That trim, shining little black head of her! Those black eyebrows like little wings! Those fan-lashed velvety eyes! That dimple just below the red delightful mouth of her! That creamy throat above the linen collar of her pretty green sweater! A thoroughbred, every inch of her! Acres of family behind her. Showed her knees too much, of course. But at any rate they were knees that could be shown.

"My watch isn't wrong," he shouted. Dr. Dimma always believed that if he contradicted loud enough, people would be convinced. "Here I am, worn out after a sleepless night, and in a hurry to get down to the hospital. Do you realize that I have an important consultation at ten? And you keep me waiting for hours for my breakfast!"

Merle didn't ask why he didn't go ahead without her. She knew no meal had any pleasure for him if she were not facing him across the table. To him she was not only Merle – she was youth, beauty, mystery, romance – everything that had deserted the life of a rotund, bald-headed, elderly doctor. Instead, she went round and kissed him.

"Now, Daddy dearest, don't be cross," she pleaded.

Generally this placated the doctor. He liked to feel that his womenkind felt the need of placating him. But the iron had bitten too deeply. A fiddle at three o'clock played by a nobody! "Caught any yet?"

"Never mind standing there in a skirt that is a sheer impertinence. Go and sit down."

Merle sat meekly enough. Trouble of some kind was brewing. Perhaps she, too, had heard the fiddle! And understood better than the doctor what had been played.

"Did I," said Dr. Dimma impressively, "see you throwing a rose at that fellow next door last night?"

"You're only asking that for rhetorical effect, Daddy," said Merle coolly. "Of course you saw me throw a rose."

Dr. Dimma snorted ironically.

"Of course," he mimicked. "Well, this has got to stop."

"What has got to stop?"

"Everything – everything. I won't have you running round with that fellow. We don't know him."

"I do," said Merle.

"Ah, you do. What do you know about him, miss? What's his pedigree?"

"Daddy dear, he isn't a horse. He's very nice. He plays a beautiful game – such a pity you don't care for golf, Daddy – and – and – perhaps he's your future son-in-law. So you really ought to know him."

Dr. Dimma glared at her and banged the table. He knew Merle was only trying to tease him, but still!

"Son-in-law! No, thank you!" The doctor's sarcasm was terrible. "No son-in-law for me who plays the fiddle when decent people should be asleep."

"But, Daddy, he was overseas and he's been subject to insomnia ever since. Besides, it helps him to think."

"Oh, blame everything on the war. That fellow never smelled powder. As for thinking – don't tell me he thinks. A he-doll like that couldn't even try to think."

"You're unjust, Daddy. It isn't his fault that he's good-looking. And – and," Merle added dreamily, "you have no idea how divinely he can kiss!"

Dr. Dimma almost choked over the mouthful of coffee he had just taken in.

"What do you know – has he dared – has he dared –"

"Daddy, you'll have apoplexy. Now, dearest, stop spluttering. I haven't made up my mind yet that I really want him. But he's such a relief after Clark."

"What's the matter with Clark?" glared Dr. Dimma. "He's clever and rich and good-looking, isn't he? And he'll make you an affectionate husband."

"An affectionate husband. Oh, Daddy, you're so Victorian," groaned Merle. "Affectionate husbands are outmoded. We like the cavemen. The only thing I really have against Clark is the fact that his face demands side-whiskers a generation too late."

"Look here, Merle, I'm serious and I want you to be. You've got to stop associating with this – this –"

"His name is –"

"I know his name. It's all I do know about him, except the self-evident fact that he's an idler and a –"

"He's been –"

"Not a word. The Dimmas have been in Sangamo for six generations. You'll be good enough to remember what I say, Merle. I mean every word of it. And you'll find I'm firm."

Merle stood up. It was time to put an end to the interview. She felt a little anxious, though she didn't show it. There had been one or two times in her life when she couldn't wheedle her father. When Dr. Dimma really did make up his mind on any point, he had never been known to change it. And she knew his reverence for ancestry and pedigrees only too well.

"You'd be more convincing, Daddy love, if you weren't so cross. Being a tyrant isn't being firm, you know. Now, don't let's quarrel this lovely morning."

"Merle, remember what I say –"

"Of course I'll remember it. How can I help remembering when you're shouting at me like that? And glaring! You're such a nice-looking father when you don't glare. I've tried to bring you up properly, darling, but I can't seem to break you of glaring. Now, run along to your little hospital. I'm going out to the club with the Benson girls. We're the committee for the dance tomorrow night, you know."

Dr. Dimma snorted again. He didn't approve of the Benson

girls – though their pedigree equalled the Dimmas'. But for that matter he approved of none of those silky sophisticated creatures Merle ran with – snaky, hipless things, with shingle bobs, and mouths that looked as if they had been making a meal of blood, and legs that might as well be naked; who powdered their noses publicly with the engaging unconcern of a cat washing its face in the gaze of thousands. Where were the girls of yesteryear? Girls that were girls – ah! But times had changed. Still, had a father no rights at all? This was all it came to – all your years of sacrifice and care. They flouted you – just flouted you in their slim insolence. Well, he'd show them – he'd show her, the darned little fool, playing fast and loose with a man like Clark Fairweather. It was time somebody brought her up with a round turn, even an outmoded father who had worshipped her and slaved for her, and was now told for his reward that a man he objected to could kiss divinely!

ONE MORNING two weeks later Dr. Dimma, who had had a sick call in the night and was very tired, decided to make a morning of it in bed. He told Merle so, rather grumpily, when she came in to see him. Being tired, even after such a night, meant that he was growing old, and he didn't like it. Especially when he had no son to carry on his work. Or son-in-law. Dr. Dimma groaned. But he looked proudly at Merle, who was off to the club again on committee work about another dance. The whole world, reflected Dr. Dimma, was dancing mad. But Merle was looking especially pretty in a smart little hat of black velvet pulled down over her laughing eyes, with two tiny winglike things sticking up at the sides as if black butterflies had alighted there. Hats had degenerated like everything else, but he rather liked this one of Merle's.

"I won't be home till after the dance, Dad, but I've told Mrs. Mason just what to get for your lunch. You're to have tomato and watercress salad if you're good and, of course, you're dining with Janes. I hope you'll have a lovely rest. What nifty pyjamas, Dad! New ones? I never saw such wonderful pyjamas."

"Where have you seen so many pyjamas?" said Dr. Dimma testily.

"On the counters," retorted Merle, crushing Dr. Dimma's vulgar mind, and tripped off jauntily.

Dr. Dimma looked after her proudly. She was a good little scout. She had taken his decree concerning Arthur Binns like a thoroughbred. There had been no more roses and golf. To be sure, she had asked him prettily two days ago if he couldn't see his way clear to knowing his neighbours. But the doctor flattered himself he had made his final decision clear to her. And she had behaved very well about it – very well.

The doctor slept the sleep of the just all the morning, had his lunch served to him in bed by Mrs. Mason, who had waited on him and adored him for twenty years, ate his favourite salad, gave Mrs. Mason a genial permission to spend the afternoon with a friend, and decided he would stay in bed till four. That would give him just time to dress and get down to the hospital in time for that consultation with Dr. Janes at five. Secretly, Dr. Dimma was inordinately proud of being asked to consult with the great Janes, who was indubitably the most eminent neurologist in the province.

What was that? At a bound Dr. Dimma was out of bed and at the window. Gracious Peter! Pigs in his rose garden – pigs – three of them. Where on earth had they come from? Up from that back street where the Kellys lived. Pigs – he'd show them . . .

The doctor flew downstairs and out over the lawn in a tantrum. The pigs saw him coming and, not liking orange-and-purple pyjamas perhaps, rushed madly through the open gate in the hedge between the doctor's property and Miss Jackson's. The doctor pursued them bravely. It wouldn't do to chase them into Miss Jackson's garden and leave them there.

The terrified porkers tore around her house, through her vegetable garden, and made their escape through a hole in the paling behind the garage. The doctor turned in triumph. He'd teach those miserable Kellys a lesson. This was what came of living just outside the town limits where people could keep any kind of nuisances. By gad, he'd move, that he would. Never mind if he had lived at Beechhurst all his life and his father before him. Sentiment was all very well – but fiddles – and pigs – and nobodies from nowhere who had never heard of a streptococcus and probably thought the violet ray was the name of a girl. Who had left that gate open? Who – it was at this point the doctor saw the dog.

Saw him so near that the whole world seemed filled with him. A bulldog – the hugest and ugliest bulldog Dr. Dimma had ever seen. A dog who evidently had a quiet taste in pyjamas.

Dr. Dimma turned, and stood not on the order of his going. The door of Miss Jackson's garage was open, and Dr. Dimma dashed in, with the dog an inch behind. There was a ladder set up against the beam of a floorless little loft, and Dr. Dimma sprinted up it as nimbly as a pussycat, pyjamas and all. He not only climbed it, but scrambled off it onto the beam. Ordinarily dogs could not climb ladders, but who knew what a devil like this could do? The doctor was taking no chances. If the dog attempted to climb the ladder he would hurl the ladder to the floor.

The dog, however, showed no inclination to climb the ladder. He sat down on his haunches and looked up at the doctor, sitting above his head in those violent pyjamas. There was a look about him that Dr. Dimma did not like – the look of a dog with any amount of spare time.

Here was a fix! How on earth was he to get down? Well, the only thing to do was to yell. Somebody would hear him – Mrs. Mason – no, Mrs. Mason had gone, and anyway he didn't want the poor old lady chewed up by the dog. That Binns nobody?

Was the dog his? Dr. Dimma suddenly realized his pyjamas. In his early wrath and late terror he had not thought of how he was dressed. Still, pyjamas or no pyjamas, he must get down. So he yelled.

A young man was standing in the garage door – a tall young man, with grey eyes and a tremendous mop of red hair. An amused young man, leaning nonchalantly against the jamb and looking not at the doctor, but at his pyjamas.

"Look here, sir," said the doctor, as soon as he got enough breath to say it, "I want you to call off your dog."

"Why should I?" the young man said coolly.

The doctor stared at him. "Why should you? Why – why –"

"Yes, why should I?" repeated the young man. "There have been tramps around here lately stealing chickens."

"Tramp, tramp. Do you take me for a tramp – or a chicken thief?"

"One never knows. Or you may have escaped from Dr. Mayberry's private asylum. Those pyjamas of yours rather lend strength to that theory. Anyhow, I understand that I haven't the pleasure of your acquaintance and I'm not taking any chances."

Dr. Dimma stared at Arthur Binns for a moment or two and, not being a stupid man, understood several things at once. So Merle had told him already. And this was his revenge.

"Young man –"

"My name is –"

"I don't care what your name is. I know what you are, to play a cowardly trick like this on an old man."

"An old man? With those pyjamas? Tut, tut!"

"Mr. Binns, this has gone far enough. Be good enough to call off your dog at once. I've an important consultation at five."

Mr. Binns shook his red head slowly and sorrowfully.

"The asylum, beyond doubt. I thought so as soon as I saw those pyjamas. Keep an eye on him, Alphonso. He may be violent."

Alphonso was keeping two eyes on him. Mr. Binns turned and walked away.

"Hey, you!" shouted the doctor incredulously. "You're not going to leave me here!"

The lean red fox – aye, that was the name for him – turned.

"I must. I can't have strangers prowling about my aunt's garage. If I knew you, of course, it might be different."

Dr. Dimma knew perfectly well what was being put up to him. And he had no intention of surrendering. No, he would die there first, pyjamas and all.

"I'm going down that ladder," he announced defiantly. "And if your dog injures me you will be held responsible for the consequences."

"Oh, but that wouldn't bring you back to life," smiled Mr. Binns. "I really wouldn't advise you to try climbing down the ladder. Alphonso is by way of being a one-man dog. Why not, instead, try enlarging the circle of your acquaintance? I'm a decent lot. I go to bed early at least once a week, and I never say anything to my friends' faces that I wouldn't say behind their backs. What say?"

"My dear young man" – oh, the contempt Dr. Dimma put into the words – "when I say a thing I mean it."

"So do I. We have at least that much in common," and Mr. Binns walked away. Before he disappeared he turned and said, "If you should happen to change your mind, I'll not be far off."

Dr. Dimma took a handkerchief out of his pyjama coat pocket and wiped his damp brow. What a devilish predicament! And that appointment with Janes at five! He must not miss it – by the nine gods of Clusium he must not. But how could he get down? There was no way but by the ladder. It was all very well to talk of going down the ladder, but the doctor knew he couldn't do it. People were sometimes literally torn to pieces by dogs, weren't they? Hadn't he read not long ago of a dog killing a man by biting into his jugular vein? He wished he did know Arthur Binns – and his whole family.

The doctor put a foot on the ladder and Alphonso made a most blood-curdling sound. The doctor hastily drew his foot back, while perspiration sprang out of every pore. There was a lot of silence. It was frightfully hot in the loft. He could hear laughter somewhere down the back street. How dared anybody laugh? And that young devil was playing his fiddle! Everything seemed to be going on as usual outside. It was indecent that it should be so. Why didn't somebody miss him? But who was there to miss him – poor old Dr. Dimma who was of no importance to anyone – except a few miserable sick people who would die if he didn't get to see them. Why didn't somebody come? People were always somewhere else when you wanted them, and when you didn't you just fell over them. Why was his daughter getting up dances at the Sangamo Club, instead of being home looking after her poor old father who was perishing of thirst in Miss Jackson's garage? He was thirsty. How many hours could that devil of a dog hang on? Would he never get thirsty? Why had he told the S.P.C.A. to get after old Dan Kelly for kicking his dog? No doubt the dog deserved to be kicked. Every dog did – just for being a dog.

Wasn't that a queer throbbing in the back of his neck? He must be calm. Yes, even though Janes – Dr. Dimma gave himself up to hate, and hated everything living or dead. He hoped Alphonso would take mange, distemper, worms, be run over by a truck, and poisoned with strychnine. He invented several more terrible deaths for Alphonso and for his master. How delightful it would be to have Arthur Binns tied to a stake, and amuse oneself throwing sharp hatchets at him! Why had Cesare Borgia been so misunderstood?

He had a sudden wild pang of hope when a black cat

walked calmly through the garage. Surely Alphonso would chase the cat – any proper dog would. Kipling said so. But Alphonso continued to squat on his hambones, with his bandy legs planted in front of him, and his unwinking eyes fastened on the purple-and-orange pyjamas, until the cat had vanished. Well, he had never had any opinion of Kipling.

Every time Dr. Dimma squirmed, Alphonso made that dreadful sound. So the doctor tried to keep perfectly still. The narrow beam was not a comfortable place to sit. His left leg went to sleep. It was an infernal sensation. How long had he been there? It must have been hours. Janes would never forgive him! Suppose he fell asleep or fainted from hunger and tumbled off the beam. Suppose he had a stroke of apoplexy or a heart failure. Suppose the dog went mad this hot day. But still it never occurred to Dr. Dimma that he knew Arthur Binns.

Again he felt a faint flicker of hope. Through the tiny window at the end of the loft he could see a portion of his own front walk. A lady came up it. Surely – surely – when she found no one at home and the front door wide open, she would have the sense to investigate a bit. Then she turned her head. Even at that distance Dr. Dimma knew her and shrank into himself. The abominable Mrs. Slocum – the awful she-reporter of the Sangamo *Banner*. His pet aversion – the only woman on earth he really detested. Mrs. Slocum, who persisted in talking to him glibly of compulsion neuroses and anxiety neuroses and inferiority complexes and such like new-fangled twaddle. Mrs. Slocum, who went in for spiritualism, and believed she had a "spirit love" on "the other side." Mrs. Slocum, who wrote up everything, big and little, for her infernal "column." What on earth was she after? If she should find him! Dr. Dimma would have sat on that beam forever – he would have run the gauntlet of forty Alphonsos rather than have Mrs. Slocum's small, pale, watery eyes light upon him in his pyjamas perched on a beam in Mrs. Jackson's garage. Suppose it got into the paper! Ridicule would be his portion all the rest of his life. He dared not draw a free breath for half an hour after he had seen her going back down the walk.

Really, that dog's eyes would be sprained! Had he ever moved them once? Dr. Dimma tried to outstare him – hadn't he read something somewhere about the power of the human eye over animals? No animal can continue to look a human being steadily in the eye. All pish-posh. Alphonso gave back stare for stare. Dr. Dimma tried "willing" him to go and "willed" hard. Alphonso merely grinned at him. Wasn't there some Master Word which if uttered would make a dog fawn at your feet? Scat – no, that was how you talked to cats.

IT MUST BE long after five now. Janes would have given him up in wrath and contempt. Never would he have the chance of such an honour again. And no doubt the Kelly pigs had returned and were rooting up his finest roses. Dr. Dimma groaned and once more felt for his handkerchief to mop his face. It was not in his pocket – it had slipped to the floor, but his fingers encountered a small scrap of paper torn from a Toronto periodical he had been reading two nights ago. A paragraph about some new rose. But on the reverse were some "society" items, and one of them leaped out and caught Dr. Dimma's staring eyes.

> Dr. A. W. Binns, the author of the famous monograph on tropical diseases, is spending the summer months in his aunt's cottage in Sangamo, where he hopes to be able to finish his essay on tuberculosis, to be entered for competition for the Carmody prize open to the world. The distinguished young Canadian, who has already won such laurels for himself and such honour for his native land, has accepted a position in Johns Hopkins and will take up his duties this autumn, etc., etc.

Dr. Dimma almost fell off the beam. He knew Arthur Binns at last! The excited yelp that he emitted could have been heard half a mile. It brought Binns to the garage door in a second.

"Feel any better acquainted with mc now?" he drawled. "Think you know me?"

"Know you," bellowed the doctor, "I've known you for years. Author of that amazing monograph on tropical diseases. What do you mean by never telling me you were A. W. Binns?"

"Oh!" Dr. Binns saw the clipping waved in Dr. Dimma's agitated hand. "So that's what brought you to a nodding acquaintance. Well, I'm not much to advertise, and I didn't think Merle would be any more likely to fall in love with me because I wrote that monograph." He did not add, "And I thought you needed a lesson," but perhaps it would not have mattered much if he had.

"You could have saved me a very uncomfortable afternoon if you hadn't been quite so modest," grunted Dr. Dimma. "Lucky that clipping happened to be in my pocket. I'd have sat here till kingdom come before I'd have knuckled down to you otherwise. Now, hadn't you better call off that – your dog?"

"Alphonso," said Dr. Binns, "this is a good friend of ours. Call it a day."

Dr. Dimma could have sworn he saw Alphonso wink at him. He did not care. He was too wild with excitement and delight to care for anything like that. What a distinguished face that fellow had! What a chin! What incredible luck that Merle had captured him! Merle, the little fool, who hadn't yet made up her mind that she "really wanted" him! Heaven grant him patience! "My son-in-law, Dr. A. W. Binns" – oh, he would die of pride!

"You'd better come down, sir, Alphonso won't touch you

now. He's really a broth of a dog. You'll think so when you know him better."

Dr. Dimma had his doubts about this. He felt he knew Alphonso quite well enough now, and he still felt he would enjoy spanking him with a board. But henceforth even Alphonso was sacrosanct.

"I'll come down if I can restore the circulation," he said, rubbing his leg. "By the way, what time is it? I had an appointment with Janes at five."

"It's a quarter to five," said Dr. Binns. "Five minutes for you to dress – ten for me to take you there. We'll make it, though we may have to knock over a few foolish pedestrians."

Dr. Dimma crept down the ladder more slowly than he had gone up it, keeping a wary eye on Alphonso. Then he held out his hand to Dr. Binns.

"I suppose you'll tell this as a good joke everywhere for years," he said ruefully.

"Oh, no," said Dr. Binns, taking his hand. "We'll keep this in the family. I don't want my father-in-law held up to ridicule. You see, Merle and I were married yesterday afternoon."

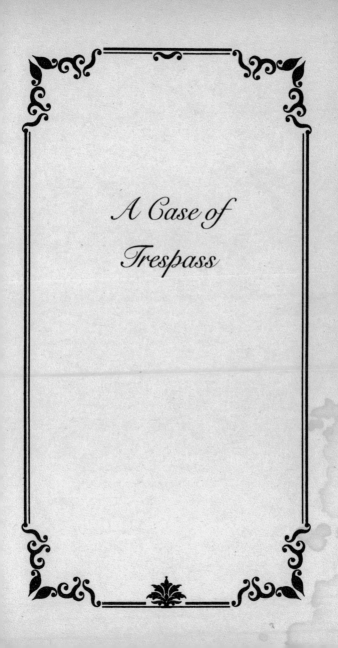

A Case of

Trespass

I T WAS THE forenoon of a hazy, breathless day, and Dan Phillips was trouting up one of the back creeks of the Carleton pond. It was somewhat cooler up the creek than out on the main body of water, for the tall birches and willows, crowding down to the brim, threw cool, green shadows across it and shut out the scorching glare, while a stray breeze now and then rippled down the wooded slopes, rustling the beech leaves with an airy, pleasant sound.

Out in the pond the glassy water creamed and shimmered in the hot sun, unrippled by the faintest breath of air. Across the soft, pearly tints of the horizon blurred the smoke of the big factory chimneys that were owned by Mr. Walters, to whom the pond and adjacent property also belonged.

Mr. Walters was a comparative stranger in Carleton, having but recently purchased the factories from the heirs of the previous owner; but he had been in charge long enough to establish a reputation for sternness and inflexibility in all his business dealings.

One or two of his employees, who had been discharged by him on what they deemed insufficient grounds, helped to deepen the impression that he was an unjust and arbitrary man, merciless to all offenders, and intolerant of the slightest infringement of his cast-iron rules.

Dan Phillips had been on the pond ever since sunrise. The trout had risen well in the early morning, but as the day wore on, growing hotter and hotter, they refused to bite, and for half an hour Dan had not caught one.

He had a goodly string of them already, however, and he surveyed them with satisfaction as he rowed his leaky little skiff to the shore of the creek.

"Pretty good catch," he soliloquized. "Best I've had this summer, so far. That big spotted one must weigh near a pound. He's a beauty. They're a good price over at the hotels now, too. I'll go home and get my dinner and go straight over with them. That'll leave me time for another try at them about sunset. Whew, how hot it is! I must take Ella May home a bunch of them blue flags. They're real handsome!"

He tied his skiff under the crowding alders, gathered a big bunch of the purple flag lilies with their silky petals, and started homeward, whistling cheerily as he stepped briskly along the fern-carpeted wood path that wound up the hill under the beeches and firs.

He was a freckled, sunburned lad of thirteen years. His neighbours all said that Danny was "as smart as a steel trap," and immediately added that they wondered where he got his smartness from – certainly not from his father!

The elder Phillips had been denominated "shiftless and slack-twisted" by all who ever had any dealings with him in his unlucky, aimless life – one of those improvident, easy-going souls who sit contentedly down to breakfast with a very faint idea where their dinner is to come from.

When he had died, no one had missed him, unless it were his patient, sad-eyed wife, who bravely faced her hard lot, and toiled unremittingly to keep a home for her two children – Dan and a girl two years younger, who was a helpless cripple, suffering from some form of spinal disease.

Dan, who was old and steady for his years, had gone manfully to work to assist his mother. Though he had been disappointed in all his efforts to obtain steady employment, he was active and obliging, and earned many a small amount by odd jobs around the village, and by helping the Carleton farmers in planting and harvest.

For the last two years, however, his most profitable source of summer income had been the trout pond. The former owner had allowed anyone who wished to fish in his pond, and Dan made a regular business of it, selling his trout at the big hotels over at Mosquito Lake. This, in spite of its unattractive name, was a popular summer resort, and Dan always found a ready market for his catch.

When Mr. Walters purchased the property it somehow never occurred to Dan that the new owner might not be so complaisant as his predecessor in the matter of the best trouting pond in the country.

To be sure, Dan often wondered why it was the pond was so deserted this summer. He could not recall having seen a single person on it save himself. Still, it did not cross his mind that there could be any particular reason for this.

He always fished up in the cool, dim creeks, which long experience had taught him were best for trout, and came and went by a convenient wood path; but he had no thought of concealment in so doing. He would not have cared had all Carleton seen him.

He had done very well with his fish so far, and prices for trout at the Lake went up every day. Dan was an enterprising boy, and a general favourite with the hotel owners. They knew that he could always be depended on.

Mrs. Phillips met him at the door when he reached home. "See, Mother," said Dan exultantly, as he held up his fish. "Just look at that fellow, will you? A pound if he's an ounce! I ought to get a good price for these, I can tell you. Let me have my dinner now, and I'll go right over to the Lake with them."

"It's a long walk for you, Danny," replied his mother pityingly, "and it's too hot to go so far. I'm afraid you'll get sunstruck or something. You'd better wait till the cool of the evening. You're looking real pale and thin this while back."

"Oh, I'm all right, Mother," assured Dan cheerfully. "I don't mind the heat a bit. A fellow must put up with some inconveniences. Wait till I bring home the money for these fish. And I mean to have another catch tonight. It's you that's looking tired. I wish you didn't have to work so hard, Mother.

If I could only get a good place you could take it easier. Sam French says that Mr. Walters wants a boy up there at the factory, but I know I wouldn't do. I ain't big enough. Perhaps something will turn up soon though. When our ship comes in, Mother, we'll have our good times."

He picked up his flags and went into the little room where his sister lay.

"See what I've brought you, Ella May!" he said, as he thrust the cool, moist clusters into her thin, eager hands. "Did you ever see such beauties?"

"Oh, Dan, how lovely they are! Thank you ever so much! If you are going over to the Lake this afternoon, will you please call at Mrs. Henny's and get those nutmeg geranium slips she promised me? Just look how nice my others are growing. The pink one is going to bloom."

"I'll bring you all the geranium slips at the Lake, if you like. When I get rich, Ella May, I'll build you a big conservatory, and I'll get every flower in the world in it for you. You shall just live and sleep among posies. Is dinner ready, Mother? Trouting's hungry work, I tell you. What paper is this?"

He picked up a folded newspaper from the table.

"Oh, that's only an old Lake *Advertiser*," answered Mrs. Phillips, as she placed the potatoes on the table and wiped her moist, hot face with the corner of her gingham apron. "Letty Mills brought it in around a parcel this morning. It's four weeks old, but I kept it to read if I ever get time. It's so seldom we see a paper of any kind nowadays. But I haven't looked at it yet. Why, Danny, what on earth is the matter?"

For Dan, who had opened the paper and glanced over the first page, suddenly gave a choked exclamation and turned pale, staring stupidly at the sheet before him.

"See, Mother," he gasped, as she came up in alarm and looked over his shoulder. This is what they read:

Anyone found fishing on my pond at Carleton after date will be prosecuted according to law, without respect of persons.

June First.   H. C. Walters.

"Oh, Danny, what does it mean?"

Dan went and carefully closed the door of Ella May's room before he replied. His face was pale and his voice shaky.

"Mean? Well, Mother, it just means that I've been stealing Mr. Walters's trout all summer – *stealing* them. That's what it means."

"Oh, Danny! But you didn't know."

"No, but I ought to have remembered that he was the new owner, and have asked him. I never thought. Mother, what does 'prosecuted according to law' mean?"

"I don't know, I'm sure, Danny. But if this is so, there's only one thing to be done. You must go straight to Mr. Walters and tell him all about it."

"Mother, I don't dare to. He is a dreadfully hard man. Sam French's father says –"

"I wouldn't believe a word Sam French's father says about Mr. Walters!" said Mrs. Phillips firmly. "He's got a spite against him because he was dismissed. Besides, Danny, it's the only right thing to do. You know that. We're poor, but we have never done anything underhand yet."

"Yes, Mother, I know," said Dan, gulping his fear bravely down. "I'll go, of course, right after dinner. I was only scared at first. I'll tell you what I'll do. I'll clean these trout nicely and take them to Mr. Walters, and tell him that, if he'll only give me time, I'll pay him back every cent of money I got for all I sold this summer. Then maybe he'll let me off, seeing as I didn't know about the notice."

"I'll go with you, Danny."

"No, I'll go alone, Mother. You needn't go with me," said Dan heroically. To himself he said that his mother had troubles enough. He would never subject her to the added ordeal of an interview with the stern factory owner. He would beard the lion in his den himself, if it had to be done.

"Don't tell Ella May anything about it. It would worry her. And don't cry, Mother, I guess it'll be all right. Let me have my dinner now and I'll go straight off."

Dan ate his dinner rapidly; then he carefully cleaned his trout, put them in a long basket, with rhubarb leaves over them, and started with an assumed cheerfulness very far from his real feelings.

He had barely passed the gate when another boy came shuffling along – a tall, raw-boned lad, with an insinuating smile and shifty, cunning eyes. The newcomer nodded familiarly to Dan.

"Hello, sonny. Going over to the Lake with your catch, are you? You'll fry up before you get there. There'll be nothing left of you but a crisp."

"No, I'm not going to the Lake. I'm going up to the factory to see Mr. Walters."

Sam French gave a long whistle of surprise.

"Why, Dan, what's taking you there? You surely ain't thinking of trying for that place, are you? Walters wouldn't look at you. Why, he wouldn't take *me*! You haven't the ghost of a chance."

"No, I'm not going for that. Sam, did you know that Mr. Walters had a notice in the Lake *Advertiser* that nobody could fish in his pond this summer?"

"Course I did – the old skinflint! He's too mean to live, that's what. He never goes near the pond himself. Regular dog in the manger, he is. Dad says –"

"Sam, why didn't you tell me about that notice?"

"Gracious, didn't you know? I s'posed everybody did, and here I've been taking you for the cutest chap this side of sunset – fishing away up in that creek where no one could see you, and cutting home through the woods on the sly. You don't mean to tell me you never saw that notice?"

"No, I didn't. Do you think I'd have gone near the pond if I had? I never saw it till today, and I'm going straight to Mr. Walters now to tell him about it."

Sam French stopped short in the dusty road and stared at Dan in undisguised amazement.

"Dan Phillips," he ejaculated, "have you plum gone out of your mind? Boy alive, you needn't be afraid that I'd peach on you. I'm too blamed glad to see anyone get the better of that old Walters, smart as he thinks himself. Gee! To dream of going to him and telling him you've been fishing in his pond! Why, he'll put you in jail. You don't know what sort of a man he is. Dad says –"

"Never mind what your dad says, Sam. My mind's made up."

"Dan, you chump, listen to me. That notice says 'prosecuted according to law.' Why, Danny, he'll put you in prison, or fine you, or something dreadful."

"I can't help it if he does," said Danny stoutly. "You get out of here, Sam French, and don't be trying to scare me. I mean to be honest, and how can I be if I don't own up to Mr. Walters that I've been stealing his trout all summer?"

"Stealing, fiddlesticks! Dan, I used to think you were a chap with some sense, but I see I was mistaken. You ain't done no harm. Walters will never miss them trout. If you're so dreadful squeamish that you won't fish no more, why, you needn't. But just let the matter drop and hold your tongue about it. That's *my* advice."

"Well, it isn't my mother's, then. I mean to go by *hers*. You needn't argue no more, Sam. I'm going."

"Go, then!" said Sam, stopping short in disgust. "You're a big fool, Dan, and serve you right if Walters lands you off to jail; but I don't wish you no ill. If I can do anything for your family after you're gone, I will, and I'll try and give your remains Christian burial – if there are any remains. So long, Danny! Give my love to old Walters!"

Dan was not greatly encouraged by this interview. He shrank more than ever from the thought of facing the stern factory owner. His courage had almost evaporated when he entered the office at the factory and asked shakily for Mr. Walters.

"He's in his office there," replied the clerk, "but he's very busy. Better leave your message with me."

"I must see Mr. Walters himself, please," said Dan firmly, but with inward trepidation.

The clerk swung himself impatiently from his stool and ushered Dan into Mr. Walters's private office.

"Boy to see you, sir," he said briefly, as he closed the ground-glass door behind him.

Dan, dizzy and trembling, stood in the dreaded presence. Mr. Walters was writing at a table covered with a businesslike litter of papers. He laid down his pen and looked up with a frown as the clerk vanished. He was a stern-looking man with deep-set grey eyes and a square, clean-shaven chin. There was not an ounce of superfluous flesh on his frame, and his voice and manner were those of the decided, resolute, masterful man of business.

He pointed to a capacious leather chair and said concisely, "What is your business with me, boy?"

Dan had carefully thought out a statement of facts beforehand, but every word had vanished from his memory. He had only a confused, desperate consciousness that he had a theft to confess and that it must be done as soon as possible. He did not sit down.

"Please, Mr. Walters," he began desperately, "I came to tell you – your notice – I never saw it before – and I've been fishing on your pond all summer – but I didn't know – honest

– I've brought you all I caught today – and I'll pay back for them all – some time."

An amused, puzzled expression crossed Mr. Walters's non-committal face. He pushed the leather chair forward.

"Sit down, my boy," he said kindly. "I don't quite understand this somewhat mixed-up statement of yours. You've been fishing on my pond, you say. Didn't you see my notice in the *Advertiser*?"

Dan sat down more composedly. The revelation was over and he was still alive.

"No, sir. We hardly ever see an *Advertiser*, and nobody told me. I'd always been used to fishing there, and I never thought but what it was all right to keep on. I know I ought to have remembered and asked you, but truly, sir, I didn't mean to steal your fish. I used to sell them over at the hotels. We saw the notice today, Mother and me, and I came right up. I've brought you the trout I caught this morning, and – if only you won't prosecute me, sir, I'll pay back every cent I got for the others – every cent, sir – if you'll give me time."

Mr. Walters passed his hand across his mouth to conceal something like a smile.

"Your name is Dan Phillips, isn't it?" he said irrelevantly, "and you live with your mother, the Widow Phillips, down there at Carleton Corners, I understand."

"Yes, sir," said Dan, wondering how Mr. Walters knew so much about him, and if these were the preliminaries of prosecution.

Mr. Walters took up his pen and drew a blank sheet towards him.

"Well, Dan, I put that notice in because I found that many people who used to fish on my pond, irrespective of leave or licence, were accustomed to lunch or camp on my property, and did not a little damage. I don't care for trouting myself; I've no time for it. However, I hardly think you'll do much damage. You can keep on fishing there. I'll give you a written permission, so that if any of my men see you they won't interfere with you. As for these trout here, I'll buy them from you at Mosquito Lake prices, and will say no more about the matter. How will that do?"

"Thank you, sir," stammered Dan. He could hardly believe his ears. He took the slip of paper Mr. Walters handed to him and rose to his feet.

"Wait a minute, Dan. How was it you came to tell me this? You might have stopped your depredations, and I should not have been any the wiser."

"That wouldn't have been honest, sir," said Dan, looking squarely at him.

There was a brief silence. Mr. Walters thrummed meditatively on the table. Dan waited wonderingly.

Finally the factory owner said abruptly, "There's a vacant place for a boy down here. I want it filled as soon as possible. Will you take it?"

"Mr. Walters! *Me*!" Dan thought the world must be turning upside down.

"Yes, you. You are rather young, but the duties are not hard or difficult to learn. I think you'll do. I was resolved not to fill that place until I could find a perfectly honest and trustworthy boy for it. I believe I have found him. I discharged the last boy because he lied to me about some trifling offence for which I would have forgiven him if he had told the truth. I can bear with incompetency, but falsehood and deceit I cannot and will not tolerate," he said, so sternly that Dan's face paled. "I am convinced that you are incapable of either. Will you take the place, Dan?"

"I will if you think I can fill it, sir. I will do my best."

"Yes, I believe you will. Perhaps I know more about you than you think. Businessmen must keep their eyes open. We'll regard this matter as settled then. Come up tomorrow at eight o'clock. And one word more, Dan. You have perhaps heard that I am an unjust and hard master. I am not the former, and you will never have occasion to find me the latter if you are always as truthful and straightforward as you have been today. You might easily have deceived me in this matter. That you did not do so is the best and only recommendation I require. Take those trout up to my house and leave them. That will do. Good afternoon."

Dan somehow got his dazed self through the glass door and out of the building. The whole interview had been such a surprise to him that he was hardly sure whether or not he had dreamed it all.

"I feel as if I were some person else," he said to himself, as he started down the hot white road. "But Mother was right. I'll stick to her motto. I wonder what Sam will say to this."

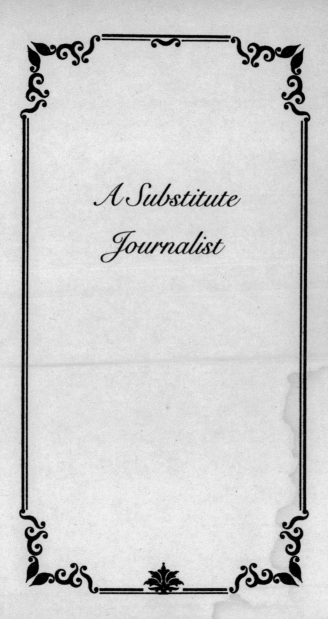

A Substitute

Journalist

LIFFORD BAXTER came into the sitting-room where Patty was darning stockings and reading a book at the same time. Patty could do things like that. The stockings were well darned too, and Patty understood and remembered what she read.

Clifford flung himself into a chair with a sigh of weariness. "Tired?" queried Patty sympathetically.

"Yes, rather. I've been tramping about the wharves all day gathering longshore items. But, Patty, I've got a chance at last. Tonight as I was leaving the office Mr. Harmer gave me a real assignment for tomorrow – two of them in fact, but only one of importance. I'm to go and interview Mr. Keefe on this new railroad bill that's up before the legislature. He's in town, visiting his old college friend, Mr. Reid, and he's quite big game. I wouldn't have had the assignment, of course, if there'd been anyone else to send, but most of the staff will be away all day tomorrow to see about that mine explosion at Midbury or the teamsters' strike at Bainsville, and I'm the only one available. Harmer gave me a pretty broad hint that it was my chance to win my spurs, and that if I worked up a good article out of it I'd stand a fair show of being taken on permanently next month when Alsop leaves. There'll be a shuffle all round then, you know. Everybody on the staff will be pushed up a peg, and that will leave a vacant space at the foot."

Patty threw down her darning needle and clapped her hands with delight. Clifford gazed at her admiringly, thinking that he had the prettiest sister in the world – she was so bright, so eager, so rosy.

"Oh, Clifford, how splendid!" she exclaimed. "Just as we'd begun to give up hope too. Oh, you must get the position! You must hand in a good write-up. Think what it means to us."

"Yes, I know." Clifford dropped his head on his hand and

stared rather moodily at the lamp. "But my joy is chastened, Patty. Of course I want to get the permanency, since it seems to be the only possible thing, but you know my heart isn't really in newspaper work. The plain truth is I don't like it, although I do my best. You know Father always said I was a born mechanic. If I only could get a position somewhere among machinery – that would be my choice. There's one vacant in the Steel and Iron Works at Bancroft – but of course I've no chance of getting it."

"I know. It's too bad," said Patty, returning to her stockings with a sigh. "I wish I were a boy with a foothold on the *Chronicle*. I firmly believe that I'd make a good newspaper woman, if such a thing had ever been heard of in Aylmer."

"That you would. You've twice as much knack in that line as I have. You seem to know by instinct just what to leave out and put in. I never do, and Harmer has to blue-pencil my copy mercilessly. Well, I'll do my best with this, as it's very necessary I should get the permanency, for I fear our family purse is growing very slim. Mother's face has a new wrinkle of worry every day. It hurts me to see it."

"And me," sighed Patty. "I do wish I could find something to do too. If only we both could get positions, everything would be all right. Mother wouldn't have to worry so. Don't say anything about this chance to her until you see what comes of it. She'd only be doubly disappointed if nothing did. What is your other assignment?"

"Oh, I've got to go out to Bancroft on the morning train and write up old Mr. Moreland's birthday celebration. He is a hundred years old, and there's going to be a presentation and speeches and that sort of thing. Nothing very exciting about it. I'll have to come back on the three o'clock train and hurry out to catch my politician before he leaves at five. Take a stroll down to meet my train, Patty. We can go out as far as Mr. Reid's house together, and the walk will do you good."

The Baxters lived in Aylmer, a lively little town with two

newspapers, the *Chronicle* and the *Ledger*. Between these two was a sharp journalistic rivalry in the matter of "beats" and "scoops." In the preceding spring Clifford had been taken on the *Chronicle* on trial, as a sort of general handyman. There was no pay attached to the position, but he was getting training and there was the possibility of a permanency in September if he proved his mettle. Mr. Baxter had died two years before, and the failure of the company in which Mrs. Baxter's money was invested had left the little family dependent on their own resources. Clifford, who had cherished dreams of a course in mechanical engineering, knew that he must give them up and go to the first work that offered itself, which he did staunchly and uncomplainingly. Patty, who hitherto had had no designs on a "career," but had been sunnily content to be a home girl and Mother's right hand, also realized that it would be well to look about her for something to do. She was not really needed so far as the work of the little house went, and the whole burden must not be allowed to fall on Clifford's eighteen-year-old shoulders. Patty was his senior by a year, and ready to do her part unflinchingly.

The next afternoon Patty went down to meet Clifford's train. When it came, no Clifford appeared. Patty stared about her at the hurrying throngs in bewilderment. Where was Clifford? Hadn't he come on the train? Surely he must have, for there was no other until seven o'clock. She must have missed him somehow. Patty waited until everybody had left the station, then she walked slowly homeward. As the *Chronicle* office was on her way, she dropped in to see if Clifford had reported there.

She found nobody in the editorial offices except the office boy, Larry Brown, who promptly informed her that not only had Clifford not arrived, but that there was a telegram from him saying that he had missed his train. Patty gasped in dismay. It was dreadful!

"Where is Mr. Harmer?" she asked.

"He went home as soon as the afternoon edition came out. He left before the telegram came. He'll be furious when he finds out that nobody has gone to interview that foxy old politician," said Larry, who knew all about Clifford's assignment and its importance.

"Isn't there anyone else here to go?" queried Patty desperately.

Larry shook his head. "No, there isn't a soul in. We're mighty short-handed just now on account of the explosion and the strike."

Patty went downstairs and stood for a moment in the hall, rapt in reflection. If she had been at home, she verily believed she would have sat down and cried. Oh, it was too bad, too disappointing! Clifford would certainly lose all chance of the permanency, even if the irate news editor did not discharge him at once. What could she do? Could she do anything? She *must* do something.

"If I only could go in his place," moaned Patty softly to herself.

Then she started. Why not? Why not go and interview the big man herself? To be sure, she did not know a great deal about interviewing, still less about railroad bills, and nothing at all about politics. But if she did her best it might be better than nothing, and might at least save Clifford his present hold.

With Patty, to decide was to act. She flew back to the reporters' room, pounced on a pencil and tablet, and hurried off, her breath coming quickly, and her eyes shining with excitement. It was quite a long walk out to Mr. Reid's place and Patty was tired when she got there, but her courage was not a whit abated. She mounted the steps and rang the bell undauntedly.

"Can I see Mr. – Mr. – Mr. –" Patty paused for a moment in dismay. She had forgotten the name. The maid who had come to the door looked her over so superciliously that Patty flushed with indignation. "The gentleman who is visiting Mr. Reid," she said crisply. "I can't remember his name, but I've come to interview him on behalf of the *Chronicle*. Is he in?"

"If you mean Mr. Reefer, he is," said the maid quite respectfully. Evidently the *Chronicle*'s name carried weight in the Reid establishment. "Please come into the library. I'll go and tell him."

Patty had just time to seat herself at the table, spread out her paper imposingly, and assume a businesslike air when Mr. Reefer came in. He was a tall, handsome old man with white hair, jet-black eyes, and a mouth that made Patty hope she wouldn't stumble on any questions he wouldn't want to answer. Patty knew she would waste her breath if she did. A man with a mouth like that would never tell anything he didn't want to tell.

"Good afternoon. What can I do for you, madam?" inquired Mr. Reefer with the air and tone of a man who means to be courteous, but has no time or information to waste.

Patty was almost overcome by the "Madam." For a moment, she quailed. She couldn't ask that masculine sphinx questions! Then the thought of her mother's pale, careworn face flashed across her mind, and all her courage came back with an inspiriting rush. She bent forward to look eagerly into Mr. Reefer's carved, granite face, and said with a frank smile:

"I have come to interview you on behalf of the *Chronicle* about the railroad bill. It was my brother who had the assignment, but he has missed his train and I have come in his place because, you see, it is so important to us. So much depends on this assignment. Perhaps Mr. Harmer will give Clifford a permanent place on the staff if he turns in a good article about you. He is only handyman now. I just couldn't let him miss

223

the chance – he might never have another. And it means so much to us and Mother."

"Are you a member of the *Chronicle* staff yourself?" inquired Mr. Reefer with a shade more geniality in his tone.

"Oh, no! I've nothing to do with it, so you won't mind my being inexperienced, will you? I don't know just what I should ask you, so won't you please just tell me everything about the bill, and Mr. Harmer can cut out what doesn't matter?"

Mr. Reefer looked at Patty for a few moments with a face about as expressive as a graven image. Perhaps he was thinking about the bill, and perhaps he was thinking what a bright, vivid, plucky little girl this was with her waiting pencil and her air that strove to be businesslike, and only succeeded in being eager and hopeful and anxious.

"I'm not used to being interviewed myself," he said slowly, "so I don't know very much about it. We're both green hands together, I imagine. But I'd like to help you out, so I don't mind telling you what I think about this bill, and its bearing on certain important interests."

Mr. Reefer proceeded to tell her, and Patty's pencil flew as she scribbled down his terse, pithy sentences. She found herself asking questions too, and enjoying it. For the first time, Patty thought she might rather like politics if she understood them – and they did not seem so hard to understand when a man like Mr. Reefer explained them. For half an hour he talked to her, and at the end of that time Patty was in full possession of his opinion on the famous railroad bill in all its aspects.

"There now, I'm talked out," said Mr. Reefer. "You can tell your news editor that you know as much about the railroad bill as Andrew Reefer knows. I hope you'll succeed in pleasing him, and that your brother will get the position he wants. But he shouldn't have missed that train. You tell him that. Boys with important things to do mustn't miss trains.

Perhaps it's just as well he did in this case though, but tell him not to let it happen again."

Patty went straight home, wrote up her interview in ship-shape form, and took it down to the *Chronicle* office. There she found Mr. Harmer, scowling blackly. The little news editor looked to be in a rather bad temper, but he nodded not unkindly to Patty. Mr. Harmer knew the Baxters well and liked them, although he would have sacrificed them all without a qualm for a "scoop."

"Good evening, Patty. Take a chair. That brother of yours hasn't turned up yet. The next time I give him an assignment, he'll manage to be on hand in time to do it."

"Oh," cried Patty breathlessly, "please, Mr. Harmer, I have the interview here. I thought perhaps I could do it in Clifford's place, and I went out to Mr. Reid's and saw Mr. Reefer. He was very kind and –"

"Mr. who?" fairly shouted Mr. Harmer.

"Mr. Reefer – Mr. Andrew Reefer. He told me to tell you that this article contained all he knew or thought about the railroad bill and –"

But Mr. Harmer was no longer listening. He had snatched the neatly written sheets of Patty's report and was skimming over them with a practised eye. Then Patty thought he must have gone crazy. He danced around the office, waving the sheets in the air, and then he dashed frantically up the stairs to the composing room.

Ten minutes later, he returned and shook the mystified Patty by the hand.

"Patty, it's the biggest beat we've ever had! We've scooped not only the *Ledger*, but every other newspaper in the country. How did you do it? How did you ever beguile or bewitch Andrew Reefer into giving you an interview?"

"Why," said Patty in utter bewilderment, "I just went out to Mr. Reid's and asked for the gentleman who was visiting there – I'd forgotten his name – and Mr. Reefer came down and I told him my brother had been detailed to interview him on behalf of the *Chronicle* about the bill, and that Clifford had missed his train, and wouldn't he let me interview him in his place and excuse my inexperience – and he did."

"It wasn't Andrew Reefer I told Clifford to interview," laughed Mr. Harmer. "It was John C. Keefe. I didn't know Reefer was in town, but even if I had I wouldn't have thought it a particle of use to send a man to him. He has never consented to be interviewed before on any known subject, and he's been especially close-mouthed about this bill, although men from all the big papers in the country have been after him. He is notorious on that score. Why, Patty, it's the biggest journalistic fish that has ever been landed in this office. Andrew Reefer's opinion on the bill will have a tremendous influence. We'll run the interview as a leader in a special edition that is under way already. Of course, he must have been ready to give the information to the public or nothing would have induced him to open his mouth. But to think that we should be the first to get it! Patty, you're a brick!"

Clifford came home on the seven o'clock train, and Patty was there to meet him, brimful of her story. But Clifford also had a story to tell and got his word in first.

"Now, Patty, don't scold until you hear why I missed the train. I met Mr. Peabody of the Steel and Iron Company at Mr. Moreland's and got into conversation with him. When he found out who I was, he was greatly interested and said Father had been one of his best friends when they were at college together. I told him about wanting to get the position in the company, and he had me go right out to the works and see about it. And, Patty, I have the place. Goodbye to the grind of newspaper items and fillers. I tried to get back to the station at Bancroft in time to catch the train but I couldn't, and it was just as well, for Mr. Keefe was suddenly summoned home this afternoon, and when the three-thirty train from town stopped at Bancroft he was on it. I found that out and I got on, going to the next station with him and getting my interview after all. It's here in my notebook, and I must hurry up to the office and hand it in. I suppose Mr. Harmer will be very much vexed until he finds that I have it."

"Oh, no. Mr. Harmer is in a very good humour," said Patty with dancing eyes. Then she told her story.

The interview with Mr. Reefer came out with glaring headlines, and the *Chronicle* had its hour of fame and glory. The next day Mr. Harmer sent word to Patty that he wanted to see her.

"So Clifford is leaving," he said abruptly when she entered the office. "Well, do you want his place?"

"Mr. Harmer, are you joking?" demanded Patty in amazement.

"Not I. That stuff you handed in was splendidly written – I didn't have to use the pencil more than once or twice. You have the proper journalist instinct all right. We need a lady on the staff anyhow, and if you'll take the place it's yours for saying so, and the permanency next month."

"I'll take it," said Patty promptly and joyfully.

"Good. Go down to the Symphony Club rehearsal this afternoon and report it. You've just ten minutes to get there," and Patty joyfully and promptly departed.

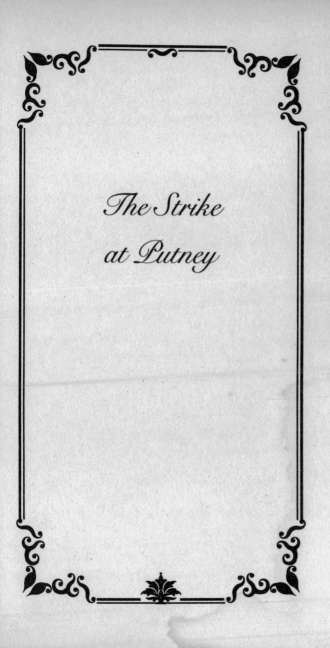

*The Strike
at Putney*

T HE CHURCH at Putney was one that gladdened the hearts of all the ministers in the presbytery whenever they thought about it. It was such a satisfactory church. While other churches here and there were continually giving trouble in one way or another, the Putneyites were never guilty of brewing up internal or presbyterial strife.

The Exeter church people were always quarrelling among themselves and carrying their quarrels to the courts of the church. The very name of Exeter gave the members of presbytery the cold creeps. But the Putney church people never quarrelled.

Danbridge church was in a chronic state of ministerlessness. No minister ever stayed in Danbridge longer than he could help. The people were too critical, and they were also noted heresy hunters. Good ministers fought shy of Danbridge, and poor ones met with a chill welcome. The harassed presbytery, worn out with "supplying," were disposed to think that the millennium would come if ever the Danbridgians got a minister whom they liked. At Putney they had had the same minister for fifteen years and hoped and expected to have him for fifteen more. They looked with horror-stricken eyes on the Danbridge theological coquetries.

Bloom Valley church was over head and heels in debt and had no visible prospect of ever getting out. The moderator said under his breath that they did over-much praying and too little hoeing. He did not believe in faith without works. Tarrytown Road kept its head above water but never had a cent to spare for missions or the schemes of the church.

In bright and shining contradistinction to these the Putney church had always paid its way and gave liberally to all departments of church work. If other springs of supply ran dry the Putneyites enthusiastically got up a "tea" or a "social," and so raised the money. Naturally the "heft" of this work fell on the women, but they did not mind – in very truth, they enjoyed it. The Putney women had the reputation of being "great church workers," and they plumed themselves on it, putting on airs at conventions among the less energetic women of the other churches.

They were especially strong on societies. There was the Church Aid Society, the Girls' Flower Band, and the Sewing Circle. There was a Mission Band and a Helping Hand among the children. And finally there was the Women's Foreign Mission Auxiliary, out of which the whole trouble grew which convulsed the church at Putney for a brief time and furnished a standing joke in presbyterial circles for years afterwards. To this day ministers and elders tell the story of the Putney church strike with sparkling eyes and subdued chuckles. It never grows old or stale. But the Putney elders are an exception. They never laugh at it. They never refer to it. It is not in the wicked, unregenerate heart of man to make a jest of his own bitter defeat.

It was in June that the secretary of the Putney W.F.M. Auxiliary wrote to a noted returned missionary who was touring the country, asking her to give an address on mission work before their society. Mrs. Cotterell wrote back saying that her brief time was so taken up already that she found it hard to make any further engagements, but she could not refuse the Putney people who were so well and favourably known in mission circles for their perennial interest and liberality. So, although she could not come on the date requested, she would, if acceptable, come the following Sunday.

This suited the Putney Auxiliary very well. On the Sunday referred to there was to be no evening service in the church owing to Mr. Sinclair's absence. They therefore appointed the missionary meeting for that night, and made arrangements to hold it in the church itself, as the classroom was too small for the expected audience.

Then the thunderbolt descended on the W.F.M.A. of

Putney from a clear sky. The elders of the church rose up to a man and declared that no woman should occupy the pulpit of the Putney church. It was in direct contravention to the teachings of St. Paul.

To make matters worse, Mr. Sinclair declared himself on the elders' side. He said that he could not conscientiously give his consent to a woman occupying his pulpit, even when that woman was Mrs. Cotterell and her subject foreign missions.

The members of the Auxiliary were aghast. They called a meeting extraordinary in the classroom and, discarding all forms and ceremonies in their wrath, talked their indignation out.

Out of doors the world basked in June sunshine and preened itself in blossom. The birds sang and chirped in the lichened maples that cupped the little church in, and peace was over all the Putney valley. Inside the classroom disgusted women buzzed like angry bees.

"What on earth are we to do?" sighed the secretary plaintively. Mary Kilburn was always plaintive. She sat on the steps of the platform, being too wrought up in her mind to sit in her chair at the desk, and her thin, faded little face was twisted with anxiety. "All the arrangements are made and Mrs. Cotterell is coming on the tenth. How can we tell her that the men won't let her speak?"

"There was never anything like this in Putney church before," groaned Mrs. Elder Knox. "It was Andrew McKittrick put them up to it. I always said that man would make trouble here yet, ever since he moved to Putney from Danbridge. I've talked and argued with Thomas until I'm dumb, but he is as set as a rock."

"I don't see what business the men have to interfere with us anyhow," said her daughter Lucy, who was sitting on one of the window-sills. "We don't meddle with them, I'm sure. As if Mrs. Cotterell would contaminate the pulpit!"

"One would think we were still in the dark ages," said Frances Spenslow sharply. Frances was the Putney school-teacher. Her father was one of the recalcitrant elders and Frances felt it bitterly – all the more that she had tried to argue with him and had been sat upon as a "child who couldn't understand."

"I'm more surprised at Mr. Sinclair than at the elders," said Mrs. Abner Keech, fanning herself vigorously. "Elders are subject to queer spells periodically. They think they assert their authority that way. But Mr. Sinclair has always seemed so liberal and broad-minded."

"You never can tell what crotchet an old bachelor will take into his head," said Alethea Craig bitingly.

The others nodded agreement. Mr. Sinclair's inveterate celibacy was a standing grievance with the Putney women.

"If he had a wife who could be our president this would never have happened, I warrant you," said Mrs. King sagely.

"But what are we going to do, ladies?" said Mrs. Robbins briskly. Mrs. Robbins was the president. She was a big, bus-tling woman with clear blue eyes and crisp, incisive ways. Hitherto she had held her peace. "They must talk themselves out before they can get down to business," she had reflected sagely. But she thought the time had now come to speak.

"You know," she went on, "we can talk and rage against the men all day if we like. They are not trying to prevent us. But that will do no good. Here's Mrs. Cotterell invited, and all the neighbouring auxiliaries notified – and the men won't let us have the church. The point is, how are we going to get out of the scrape?"

A helpless silence descended upon the classroom. The eyes of every woman present turned to Myra Wilson. Every-one could talk, but when it came to action they had a fashion of turning to Myra.

She had a reputation for cleverness and originality. She never talked much. So far today she had not said a word. She was sitting on the sill of the window across from Lucy Knox. She swung her hat on her knee, and loose, moist rings of dark hair curled around her dark, alert face. There was a sparkle in her grey eyes that boded ill to the men who were peaceably pursuing their avocations, rashly indifferent to what the women might be saying in the maple-shaded classroom.

"Have you any suggestion to make, Miss Wilson?" said Mrs. Robbins, with a return to her official voice and manner.

Myra put her long, slender index finger to her chin.

"I think," she said decidedly, "that we must strike."

WHEN ELDER KNOX went in to tea that evening he glanced somewhat apprehensively at his wife. They had had an altercation before she went to the meeting, and he supposed she had talked herself into another rage while there. But Mrs. Knox was placid and smiling. She had made his favourite soda biscuits for him and inquired amiably after his progress in hoeing turnips in the southeast meadow.

She made, however, no reference to the Auxiliary meeting, and when the biscuits and the maple syrup and two cups of matchless tea had nerved the elder up, his curiosity got the better of his prudence – for even elders are human and curiosity knows no gender – and he asked what they had done at the meeting.

"We poor men have been shaking in our shoes," he said facetiously.

"Were you?" Mrs. Knox's voice was calm and faintly amused. "Well, you didn't need to. We talked the matter over very quietly and came to the conclusion that the session knew best and that women hadn't any right to interfere in church business at all."

Lucy Knox turned her head away to hide a smile. The elder beamed. He was a peace-loving man and disliked "ructions" of any sort and domestic ones in particular. Since the decision of the session Mrs. Knox had made his life a burden to him.

He did not understand her sudden change of base, but he accepted it very thankfully.

"That's right – that's right," he said heartily. "I'm glad to hear you coming out so sensible, Maria. I was afraid you'd work yourselves up at that meeting and let Myra Wilson or Alethea Craig put you up to some foolishness or other. Well, I guess I'll jog down to the Corner this evening and order that barrel of pastry flour you want."

"Oh, you needn't," said Mrs. Knox indifferently. "We won't be needing it now."

"Not needing it! But I thought you said you had to have some to bake for the social week after next."

"There isn't going to be any social."

"Not any social?"

Elder Knox stared perplexedly at his wife. A month previously the Putney church had been recarpeted, and they still owed fifty dollars for it. This, the women declared, they would speedily pay off by a big cake and ice-cream social in the hall. Mrs. Knox had been one of the foremost promoters of the enterprise.

"Not any social?" repeated the elder again. "Then how is the money for the carpet to be got? And *why* isn't there going to be a social?"

"The men can get the money somehow, I suppose," said Mrs. Knox. "As for the social, why, of course, if women aren't good enough to speak in church they are not good enough to work for it either. Lucy, dear, will you pass me the cookies?"

"Lucy dear" passed the cookies and then rose abruptly and left the table. Her father's face was too much for her.

"What confounded nonsense is this?" demanded the elder explosively.

Mrs. Knox opened her mellow brown eyes widely, as if in amazement at her husband's tone.

"I don't understand you," she said. "Our position is perfectly logical."

She had borrowed that phrase from Myra Wilson, and it floored the elder. He got up, seized his hat, and strode from the room.

That night, at Jacob Wherrison's store at the Corner, the Putney men talked over the new development. The social was certainly off – for a time, anyway.

"Best let 'em alone, I say," said Wherrison. "They're mad at us now and doing this to pay us out. But they'll cool down later on and we'll have the social all right."

"But if they don't," said Andrew McKittrick gloomily, "who is going to pay for that carpet?"

This was an unpleasant question. The others shirked it.

"I was always opposed to this action of the session," said Alec Craig. "It wouldn't have hurt to have let the woman speak. 'Tisn't as if it was a regular sermon."

"The session knew best," said Andrew sharply. "And the minister – you're not going to set your opinion up against his, are you, Craig?"

"Didn't know they taught such reverence for ministers in Danbridge," retorted Craig with a laugh.

"Best let 'em alone, as Wherrison says," said Abner Keech.

"Don't see what else we can do," said John Wilson shortly.

ON SUNDAY MORNING the men were conscious of a bare, deserted appearance in the church. Mr. Sinclair perceived it himself. After some inward wondering he concluded that it was because there were no flowers anywhere. The table before the pulpit was bare. On the organ a vase held a sorry, faded bouquet left over from the previous week. The floor was unswept. Dust lay thickly on the pulpit Bible, the choir chairs, and the pew backs.

"This church looks disgraceful," said John Robbins in an angry undertone to his daughter Polly, who was president of the Flower Band. "What in the name of common sense is the good of your Flower Banders if you can't keep the place looking decent?"

"There is no Flower Band now, Father," whispered Polly in turn. "We've disbanded. Women haven't any business to meddle in church matters. You know the session said so."

It was well for Polly that she was too big to have her ears boxed. Even so, it might not have saved her if they had been anywhere else than in church.

Meanwhile the men who were sitting in the choir – three basses and two tenors – were beginning to dimly suspect that there was something amiss here too. Where were the sopranos and the altos? Myra Wilson and Alethea Craig and several other members of the choir were sitting down in their pews with perfectly unconscious faces. Myra was looking out of the window into the tangled sunlight and shadow of the great maples. Alethea Craig was reading her Bible.

Presently Frances Spenslow came in. Frances was organist, but today, instead of walking up to the platform, she slipped demurely into her father's pew at one side of the pulpit. Eben Craig, who was the Putney singing master and felt himself responsible for the choir, fidgeted uneasily. He tried to catch Frances's eye, but she was absorbed in reading the mission report she had found in the rack, and Eben was finally forced to tiptoe down to the Spenslow pew and whisper, "Miss Spenslow, the minister is waiting for the doxology. Aren't you going to take the organ?"

Frances looked up calmly. Her clear, placid voice was audible not only to those in the nearby pews, but to the minister.

"No, Mr. Craig. You know if a woman isn't fit to speak in the church she can't be fit to sing in it either."

Eben Craig looked exceedingly foolish. He tiptoed gingerly back to his place. The minister, with an unusual flush on his thin, ascetic face, rose suddenly and gave out the opening hymn.

Nobody who heard the singing in Putney church that day ever forgot it. Untrained basses and tenors, unrelieved by a single female voice, are not inspiring.

There were no announcements of society meetings for the forthcoming week. On the way home from church that day irate husbands and fathers scolded, argued, or pleaded, according to their several dispositions. One and all met with the same calm statement that if a noble, self-sacrificing woman like Mrs. Cotterell were not good enough to speak in the Putney church, ordinary, everyday women could not be fit to take any part whatever in its work.

Sunday School that afternoon was a harrowing failure. Out of all the corps of teachers only one was a man, and he alone was at his post. In the Christian Endeavour meeting on Tuesday night the feminine element sat dumb and unresponsive. The Putney women never did things by halves.

The men held out for two weeks. At the end of that time they "happened" to meet at the manse and talked the matter over with the harassed minister. Elder Knox said gloomily, "It's this way. Nothing can move them women. I know, for I've tried. My authority has been set at naught in my own household. And I'm laughed at if I show my face in any of the other settlements."

The Sunday School superintendent said the Sunday School was going to wrack and ruin, also the Christian Endeavour. The condition of the church for dust was something scandalous, and strangers were making a mockery of the singing. And the carpet had to be paid for. He supposed they would have to let the women have their own way.

The next Sunday evening after service Mr. Sinclair arose hesitatingly. His face was flushed, and Alethea Craig always declared that he looked "just plain everyday cross." He announced briefly that the session after due deliberation had concluded that Mrs. Cotterell might occupy the pulpit on the evening appointed for her address.

The women all over the church smiled broadly. Frances Spenslow got up and went to the organ stool. The singing in the last hymn was good and hearty. Going down the steps after dismissal Mrs. Elder Knox caught the secretary of the Church Aid by the arm.

"I guess," she whispered anxiously, "you'd better call a special meeting of the Aids at my house tomorrow afternoon. If we're to get that social over before haying begins we've got to do some smart scurrying."

The strike in the Putney church was over.

Editorial Note

The stories in this collection were originally published in the following magazines and newspapers, and are listed here in alphabetical order. Where the original illustrations accompanying the stories are available, they have been included. Obvious typographical errors have been corrected, spelling and punctuation normalized.

At the Bay Shore Farm, *Forward* and *Wellspring*, 9 January 1904, 9-10.

Bessie's Doll, *Western Christian Advocate*, 11 February 1914, 12-14.

The Blue North Room, *East and West*, 21 April 1906, 121-22.

A Case of Trespass, *Golden Days*, 24 July 1897, 561-62. Also in *King's Own*, 15 May 1909, 79 (abbreviated).

Dorinda's Desperate Deed, *Days of Youth*, 9 December 1906, 2-3, 7.

The Fillmore Elderberries, *East and West*, 18 September 1909, 299, 302.

The Genesis of the Doughnut Club, *Epworth Herald*, 23 November 1907, 659-61.

How We Went to the Wedding, *Housewife*, April and May 1913, 3-5, 31; 12-13, 28. Also in *Family Herald*, 20, 27 February and 6 March 1935, 22, 34; 27; 23.

In Spite of Myself, by M. L. Cavendish, *Chicago Inter Ocean*, 5 July 1896, 37-38.

Lilian's Business Venture, *Advocate and Guardian*, 1
November 1900, 335-37.

Ned's Stroke of Business, *Farm and Fireside*, 15 January
1903, 17.

A Patent Medicine Testimonial, *Star Monthly*, April 1903,
7-8.

A Question of Acquaintance, *MacLean's*, 1 October 1929,
12-13, 81-83.

The Strike at Putney, *Western Christian Advocate*, 16
September 1903, 14-15. Also in *National Magazine*, May
1909, 193-96; and in *Westminster*, May 1914, 467-72.
Reprinted, 1985, *Guelph Alumnus*.

A Substitute Journalist, *Forward* and *Wellspring*, 9 March
1907, 73-74.

Their Girl Josie, *American Home* [1906]. Also in *MacLean's*,
July 1915, 17-19.

Where There Is a Will There Is a Way [1934; no publication
information available].

Why Mr. Cropper Changed His Mind, *Household Guest*
[1903].

Acknowledgements

The late Dr. Stuart Macdonald gave me permission to begin the research that culminated in my collection of Montgomery's stories; Professors Mary Rubio and Elizabeth Waterston encouraged and advised me; C. Anderson Silber gave his constant support. Librarians were unfailingly helpful.

L. M. Montgomery

For the most complete listing, see Russell, Russell, and Wilmshurst, *Lucy Maud Montgomery: A Preliminary Bibliography*, University of Waterloo Library Bibliography Series, No. 13 (Waterloo: University of Waterloo Library, 1986).

The "Anne" Books (in order of Anne's life)

Anne of Green Gables, 1908
Anne of Avonlea, 1909
Anne of the Island, 1915
Anne of Windy Poplars, 1936
Anne's House of Dreams, 1917
Anne of Ingleside, 1939
Rainbow Valley, 1919
Rilla of Ingleside, 1920

The "Emily" Books

Emily of New Moon, 1923
Emily Climbs, 1925
Emily's Quest, 1927

Other Novels (in chronological order)

Kilmeny of the Orchard, 1910
The Story Girl, 1911

The Golden Road, 1913
The Blue Castle, 1926
Magic for Marigold, 1929
A Tangled Web, 1931
Pat of Silver Bush, 1933
Mistress Pat, 1935
Jane of Lantern Hill, 1937

Collections of Short Stories

Chronicles of Avonlea, 1912
Further Chronicles of Avonlea, 1920
The Road to Yesterday, 1974
The Doctor's Sweetheart, and Other Stories, 1979
Akin to Anne: Tales of Other Orphans, 1988
Along the Shore: Tales by the Sea, 1989
Among the Shadows: Tales from the Darker Side, 1990
After Many Days: Tales of Time Passed, 1991

Poetry

The Watchman, and Other Poems, 1916
Poetry of Lucy Maud Montgomery, 1987